VENGEANCE TRAIL

A vengeance trail brings Waco McAllum to Santa Rosa, hunting his brother's killers: a grudge which can only be settled by blood. He finds valuable allies in Drifter, Latigo Rawlins, and Gabriel Moonlight — three men who are no strangers to trouble. But along the way, he finds himself on another trail: a crooked one that leads straight to a gang of violent cattle-rustlers. In the final showdown, will Waco get his revenge — or a whole lot more besides?

STEVE HAYES

VENGEANCE TRAIL

Complete and Unabridged

LINFORD
Leicester

First published in Great Britain in 2014

First Linford Edition
published 2016

A catalogue record for this book is available
from the British Library.

ISBN 978–1–4448–2682–1

Published by
F. A. Thorpe (Publishing)
Anstey, Leicestershire

Set by Words & Graphics Ltd.
Anstey, Leicestershire
Printed and bound in Great Britain by
T. J. International Ltd., Padstow, Cornwall

This book is printed on acid-free paper

For Chris, Georgie and Mason
This one's for you, guys

Prologue

Jonas 'Waco' McAllum stood at the bar in the old Corn Exchange Hotel, enjoying a Mule Skinner after lunch and idly watching a poker game going on at one of the nearby tables. None of the five players were professional gamblers; they were all businessmen who owned stores in Mesilla, New Mexico, and should have been working in them. Instead they were here, like kids playing hooky, arguing over a pot worth, at most, three dollars, as if their lives depended on it.

Behind the bar Eli Wykopff rolled his eyes in disbelief. A gaunt club-footed man of fifty-odd with sunken cheeks and a comb-over that resembled a spider straddling his bald head, he was a fixture in the adobe-walled cantina, having worked there for so long no one could remember exactly when he started. He was a gloomy, pessimistic bastard but everyone liked him. He was talkative if you felt like talking, silent as a ghost if you didn't. And most important of all, he always poured an honest drink. Now, as was his custom every afternoon after the Butterfield Overland stage had left, he stood rinsing and drying glasses for the night crowd that always drifted in after supper to swap lies over cheap whiskey and mescal wine.

Bored, Waco was about to leave and ride out to his brother's ranch, a small spread outside of town, when the batwing doors burst inward, followed by Tommy Riggins who entered at a dead run and stopped right in front of him, eyes saucers, red-faced and panting, so out-of-breath he couldn't suck in enough wind to get out a single word.

'Easy, young 'un,' Waco said gently. 'Take a few deep breaths . . . calm down and . . . then spit out what you come to say.'

The poker players, oblivious of Tommy, continued arguing while Wykopff draped his towel over his shoulder and limped to the end of the bar to refill a customer's beer.

'Okay,' Waco said when Tommy had calmed down enough to talk, 'what is it you want to tell me?'

'It — it's your brother, Mr. McAllum.'

'Chris — what about him?'

'These m-men, they come and they — they dragged him away.'

'What do you mean 'dragged him away'? Away from where?'

'His place . . . '

'His ranch, you mean?'

Tommy nodded, copper-colored curls bobbing, blue eyes staring up at Waco.

'Why? I mean, why'd they grab him? And who were the men? Do you know?'

'Uh-uh. Just some men wearing flour sacks over their heads. 'Leastwise, that's what the new hand at the Bar-T told me. Crochett or Crockett, I think

3

he said his name was.'

'Why'd he tell you?' Waco demanded. 'Were you over at the Bar-T?'

'No, Mr. McAllum. I was fishing down at Green Frog Creek and he stopped to water his horse, which was all wore out from running and trembling awful bad — '

'Whoa, hold on,' Waco said, cutting him off. 'Forget the horse and let's get back to my brother. This fella Crockett or Crochett told you that he saw Chris being dragged from his spread by some men. Am I right so far?'

'Y-Yes, sir.'

'And he didn't know what Chris had done or why they'd taken him?'

'Not for sure, no.'

Waco saw something in Tommy's eyes that made him uneasy. 'How about not for sure? I mean, did he have any idea at all . . . even a guess?'

Tommy didn't answer but the fear in his eyes increased.

'C'mon, boy,' Waco coaxed. 'It's all

4

right . . . you can tell me . . . I won't get sore.'

Tommy started to speak, hesitated, eyes bright with fear, and then blurted: 'Said he heard 'em say they was taking him to Fuller's Oak to lynch him for rustling.'

★   ★   ★

Waco put the spurs to his buckskin and kept it at full gallop until he'd reached the crest of the scrub-covered hill that on the other side sloped down to a ravine in which Fuller's Oak stood. By then, the horse was dead on its feet. As it labored slowly to the top it gave a shuddering, wheezing sigh, blood and foam spraying from its flared nostrils. Then it collapsed, Waco barely managing to leap clear before the buckskin hit the dirt.

Getting to his knees, he pulled his Winchester from its scabbard and crawled to the top of the hill. Keeping his head down, he looked into the ravine below. His younger brother was already astride his chestnut mare with his hands tied behind him and a rope around his neck . . . the other end of which hung over one of the dead leafless limbs of the infamous hangman's tree, Fuller's Oak.

Even as Waco looked, one of the dozen or so hooded riders gathered around Chris now nudged his blue roan forward and raised his quirt to strike the mare.

'Wait! Hold it!' Waco yelled. Jumping up, he went charging down the slope.

The hooded riders turned, surprised to see him running toward them.

The man on the blue roan barked orders to the men. They pulled out their rifles and fired into the dirt at Waco's feet, forcing him to stop before he reached them.

'Drop your rifle,' the man ordered. Then, as Waco obeyed: 'Mister, I'm giving you fair warning. Either you turn around and get back up that hill or we'll hang you too.'

'For what?' Waco demanded.

'They don't need no goddamn reason,' his brother exclaimed. 'If they did, they wouldn't be planning to stretch my neck.'

'Be reasonable, mister,' Waco said. ''Least tell me why you're hanging my brother.'

'Him and another fella — Clete Addison, who we shot as he tried to get away — were using a running iron on some beef they'd rustled — beef that already had my brand on them.'

'He's lying, J.W.,' Chris said. 'That beef didn't have his brand on 'em. They belonged to Mr. — '

Waco cut him off. 'Never mind who they belonged to! Did you rustle them?'

Chris hesitated.

'There's your goddamn answer,' said a tall, large, hooded man whose soft belly bulged over his saddle horn. 'Kid's guilty as hell!'

Waco ignored the man and stared fixedly at his brother. 'I'm waiting . . .'

7

Again Chris hesitated, as if hiding a secret he couldn't share.

'Goddammit, Chris, answer me! Did you rustle that beef?'

'It ain't as simple as yes or no,' Chris said. He nodded toward the man on the blue roan. 'Ask him. He'll tell you. Sonofabitch is just as guilty as I am.'

'Then you did rustle them?' Waco said before the man could answer.

'Course he did!' The big paunchy man leaned forward as he spoke, his coat opening to reveal the tip of a silver star pinned on his shirt. 'Why for would we want to hang him if he didn't?' Though his voice was muffled by the hood it sounded vaguely familiar to Waco.

'To make everyone think you're doing your job,' Chris replied. To Waco he added: 'You're wasting your breath, J. W. Do like they say and get the hell out of here, 'fore you end up like me.'

Waco ignored him and turned to the man on the blue roan. 'Mister, I ain't one to interfere in another man's business. But this is my kid brother and I've raised him since our folks died back in '78. And no matter whatever else he is or what trouble he's gotten into, I've never known him to flat out lie. If he says there's more to this than meets the eye, and you're part of it, I'd bet my life that he's telling it straight!'

The man studied him, eyes glittering behind the slits in the sack covering his head.

'You had your chance, mister,' he said grimly. Then to the men: 'Hang 'em both!'

1

He rode out of the desert, the late-afternoon sun hot on his back, his flat-crowned black hat pulled low over his eyes, and on entering town headed straight for Gustafson's Livery Stable.

He was a tall, wide-shouldered, lean-hipped man on the wrong side of thirty. He had a hard weathered face spattered with trail dirt, a nose that had been broken in a saloon fight and below a gunfighter's mustache thin lips that seldom smiled. But it was his eyes that everyone remembered. Gray as a wintry day, they were cold and dispassionate and crinkled at the corners from years of squinting in the sun.

As he rode along Main Street he stared straight ahead, deep in thought, but still alert. And by the jut of his jaw and his grim, tight-lipped mouth it was obvious they were not pleasant thoughts and anyone with a grain of sense would have stayed clear of him.

His horse, a leggy sorrel bred to run, was caked with sweat and labored at every step. The horse was obviously played out. But if the weary rider was aware of the animal's condition — or even cared about it — he showed no sign of it. He sat there in the saddle, erect and implacable, the reins held slackly in his strong capable hands, seemingly aware of nothing yet somehow aware of everything.

Not that the sorrel expected any sympathy from the man. They had ridden together too long not to know each other's disposition and their relationship was, at best, thorny.

With dusk approaching, most of the townspeople were home fixing supper. Those who weren't gave the stranger no more than a casual glance as he rode past and then went on about their business. It wasn't surprising. Ever since the arrival of the railroad a few years back, strangers weren't uncommon in Santa Rosa — not even a stranger with a low-slung, tied-down holster holding a blued Merwin Hulbert Frontier model .44–40 revolver with well-worn cedar grips.

But not all strangers arrived by train. Though the coming of the railroad had been responsible for Santa Rosa blossoming from an insignificant little pueblo to a town of reasonable importance, many strangers came from far-off places by wagon or horseback. Others rode up from Mexico. The border was only a short ride to the south and just across the border was Puerto Palomas. A hot, dusty, lawless pueblo, it was a haven for outlaws, gunslingers, whores and drunken border trash. None of them were welcome and all the townspeople agreed that the strangers who came from Palomas were the most dangerous strangers of all.

This stranger hadn't come from Palomas. He'd ridden in from the southeast, from Texas or beyond, which meant he'd survived the Devil's Anvil, an infamous stretch of desert so hot and arid that not even the Apaches or Comanches dared to cross it.

The fact that this man had crossed it *and* was still alive proved he was not only especially tough but perhaps a tad reckless. The few pedestrians who saw him ride by were amazed by his achievement, but at the same time they couldn't help but wonder what possible reason had driven him to attempt such a life-threatening ride.

Adding to the mystery was the fact that despite the relentless heat he'd endured, his sweat-soaked blue denim shirt was buttoned up about his throat, and knotted around the upturned collar was a dust-caked red kerchief that completely hid his neck.

Reaching the livery stable, he dismounted, stretched the stiffness from his back and led his weary horse to the water-trough beside the open double-doors. As the sorrel drank greedily, the stranger removed his hat and hung it on the saddle-horn. Then without unbuttoning his shirt, he dunked his head in the water. After a moment he straightened up and shook his head like a dog shakes after a swim, his long dark hair spraying water everywhere.

'Hey, mister,' a voice complained behind him. 'That water's for horses to drink, not to wash up in.'

The stranger, whose name was Waco McAllum, turned and eyed the gawky teenage boy standing in the door of the stable. He wasn't much to look at. In that awkward stage between youth and man, he had long straggly brown hair, a pimply sunburned face no girl would look at twice and a surly mouth. He glared defiantly at the Waco, one hand gripping a long-handled pitchfork, the sharp tines of which glinted in the fading sunlight.

Waco shrugged. 'I don't reckon the horses will mind.'

'But *I* do.'

'Then *you* change the water.'

'Like hell I will.' The boy raised the

14

pitchfork threateningly. 'I don't get paid extra for doing things twice, mister.'

'Fair enough. Here.' Waco dug a coin from his trail-worn jeans and flipped it to the hostile teenager. 'That's for your trouble.'

The boy made no attempt to catch the quarter and it fell on the dirt between his shabby scuffed boots.

'Keep your money,' he said contemptuously. 'I work for Mr. Gustafson, not you or any other wore out grub-line rider.'

Waco felt like cuffing him. But he was too tired to let an ill-mannered boy rile him. Besides, there was something about the youth that intrigued him — made him think of himself.

'Anyways,' the boy added, 'you'll be a-needing them two bits.'

'For what?'

'Graining your horse.'

'Who says I want him grained?'

'Me.'

'Oh. Know a lot about horses, do you?'

'Enough.' The boy gazed admiringly at the sweat-caked sorrel and when he next spoke he'd lost his belligerence. 'But even if I didn't it wouldn't matter none. Any fool can see a horse like that is well worth a few oats.' Turning, he went back into the stable.

Waco sourly eyed the stallion, which seemed to know it had just been complimented. 'Don't be getting a swolled head,' he warned it. 'Only thing you're worth is yesterday's coffee dregs!'

The sorrel snorted, offended, and stamped the ground with its foreleg.

Waco walked warily around the horse, making sure he was out of kicking range, and scooped up the quarter. Pocketing it, he pulled out his shirttail and dried his face and hands. He made no attempt to unbutton his shirt or remove his kerchief — or to dry his still-dripping hair. He merely ran his fingers through it, pushing it back from his tanned angular face, and jammed his hat on. Then grasping the reins, he tried to lead the horse away from the trough.

The sorrel resisted and kept on drinking.

'Idiot,' Waco grumbled, tugging on the reins. 'You want to bloat up?'

The sorrel stubbornly fought him and when Waco tugged harder, it took a swipe at him. It would have been a mean bite, but Waco was expecting it. Jumping back, he narrowly avoided the stallion's big yellow teeth.

'Damn your lousy hide,' he cursed. 'I ought to sell you for wolf bait.'

The sorrel ignored him. Having made its point, it nickered, as if pleased with itself, and let Waco lead him into the stable.

Inside, Waco found the hostler, Lars Gustafson, sitting hunched over on an upturned bucket studying a checkerboard that sat atop an empty beer keg. The game was already in progress and several of the checkers, black and red, were piled alongside the board. Another upturned keg sat unoccupied opposite the hostler.

Tying up his horse Waco stopped by the old, gray-bearded Swede, whose short squat body was crippled by gout and arthritis, and dug out money. 'How much to stall him?'

'Dollars or pesos?' Lars said without looking up.

'Dollars.'

'Be one dollar.'

'And two bits extra to grain him?'

Lars looked up, curious. 'Who tell you this?'

Waco thumbed at the boy, who was cleaning out a stall in back. 'The kid, there.'

'Mason?'

'Why so surprised?'

'Mason, he don't usually talk to no one. Not even me. Must like you, I t'ink.'

'Not me,' Waco said, 'my horse.' He counted out a dollar and a quarter and stacked the coins on the barrel top. 'Is the boy kin of yourn?'

'No. Why you ask?'

'Could sorely use some manners.'

'I say this same thing many times to his pa.'

'Obviously he didn't listen.'

'Judd, he never listen to nobody but himself.'

'Sounds familiar. Bet he never talked much either — 'cept with his fists and belt.'

Lars looked surprised. 'You knew Judd McCutcheon?'

'Uh-uh. But I was raised by a man just like him. Fortunately, he ran into a bullet a few years back, saving me and my brother and ma from any more beatings.'

'I t'ink many folks wish same thing happen to McCutcheon.'

'So why didn't someone oblige him?'

'There was talk of it.'

'But nobody had the guts to follow through?'

The Swede shrugged. 'Weren't necessary. One time after McCutcheon beat his wife bloody, he ride off and never come back.'

'Nothing like a happy ending,' Waco said. He watched the boy working. It brought back memories of his own youth and he sighed. 'Make sure there's fresh hay in the stall.'

'Always.' The old hostler studied the checkers as if figuring out his next move. 'How long you plan to stay in Santa Rosa, mister?'

'Depends on Stillman Stadtlander.'

Lars grunted in disgust. 'You work for Stadtlander?'

'Not yet.'

The old Swede lost his friendliness. 'You must pay each day in advance or you not get horse back.'

Waco wasn't surprised. This wasn't the first time Stadtlander's name had rankled someone. During the ride here from Texas he'd stopped in a cantina for a drink and mentioned the cattle baron to the barkeep. The man grabbed a scattergun from under the bar and told him to get out. Waco obeyed and continued on his way to Santa Rosa.

Now, looking at the hostler, he said:

'Don't worry, old timer. I ain't never run out on a debt yet.' About to leave, he looked at the board and pointed at one of the red checkers. 'Rules say you got to jump that.'

'Ain't my turn. It's the sheriff's.'

Waco grinned. 'All the more reason to jump it.' Grabbing his Winchester and saddlebags, he walked out before the hostler could respond.

2

Across the street, a short walk from the stable, stood the elegant Carlisle Hotel. A few doors down from it, on the corner of Main and a cross-street named Blossom, was an old but respectable two-story adobe building with a sign over the front door: *ROOMS*. Under that in smaller letters was printed: *Men/Hombres Only. No Women/Mujeres. No Drinking!*

Waco decided it was exactly what he was looking for. Crossing the street, he ducked between two horsemen and a lumbering freight-wagon and entered the rooming-house.

A girl of about ten, wearing a pale blue dress and a matching hair ribbon, sat sulking behind the front desk. She had shoulder-length hair the color of corn silk, huge violet eyes filled with curiosity and, normally, an impudent grin. Today, though, she was upset about something and looked glum.

'Room, mister?' she asked Waco.

'Please.'

The girl turned the register toward him and indicated the quill pen and ink well at his elbow. 'Make your mark.'

'How about I write my name instead?'

'Suit yourself, mister.' She watched him sign his name then said: 'You write awful pretty. Must've went to school, huh?'

'Didn't have to,' Waco said. ''Fore ma got to ailing, she was a schoolteacher, so I got my learning at home.'

The girl mulled over his reply, intrigued by the idea of home-schooling, and then remembered something. 'You read the sign by the door?'

'Wouldn't be here if I hadn't.'

'It was Momma's idea, not mine.'

'It's a good one.'

'You think? Reckon if I was a man, it would rile me something fierce.'

'How come?'

''Cause it don't make sense. If we allowed women and drinking, we'd be booked up full all the time, 'stead of always having rooms to spare. If you know what I mean?'

Waco knew exactly what she meant. 'But you'd also have to deal with drunks, fights, broken furniture, and the sheriff in your face all the time for running a bordello. And the fines you'd end up paying the court would outweigh your profits.'

The girl shrugged and wrinkled her nose as if that didn't matter. But Waco, who'd been watching her eyes, saw that neither the problems nor the fines had occurred to her.

'Got a room facing the street?' he asked.

'Which street? Blossom or Main?'

'Main.'

The girl checked the pigeon holes behind her, 'You're in luck, mister,' grabbed a key from one of them and handed it to Waco. Simultaneously, she

24

held out her other hand, palm up, and didn't remove it until Waco paid her for the room. 'Top of the stairs, far end of the hall, Mr. — uh — ' She glanced at the register. ' — McAllum.'

'Thanks, Miss — ?'

'Lockhart.'

'Got a first name, Miss Lockhart?'

The girl hesitated, reluctant to give it.

'C'mon now, it can't be that bad.'

Grudgingly the girl said: 'Danny.'

'Danny?' Waco gave a rare smile. 'That must be short for something.'

The girl glanced around, making sure they were alone before whispering: 'Daniella. But you better not call me that,' she added fiercely, 'or say anything nice about my dress or I'll hate you forever.'

'Got my word on it,' Waco said and offered her his big, weathered hand.

Danny locked gazes with him, searching his face for some kind of proof that she could trust him. She found it amid the integrity in his eyes and firmly shook his hand.

Waco didn't know why but he felt glad she'd accepted him. 'See you in the morning,' he told her and started for the stairs.

'No, you won't,' she called out. 'Momma makes me go to that dumb ol' school.'

3

Upstairs in his room Waco removed his spurs and sat beside the open window in the cool violet dusk, smoking a hand-rolled and watching the sheriff's office which was farther up Main Street.

A half-hour passed. With night approaching the horse-drawn traffic had thinned out. Most pedestrians had gone home and lights glinted in the windows of the cafes and cantinas lining both sides of the dirt street. Waco lit another smoke, picked a bit of loose tobacco from his lip and wondered if Sheriff Forbes would ever come out of his office.

When another thirty minutes passed and the lawman still hadn't appeared hunger forced Waco to buckle on his gun and leave the room.

Downstairs, a dark-haired woman in

a simple black dress was checking receipts at the front desk. Her back was to him as she counted out money. When she was finished she wrote the total in a ledger. Unhappy with the amount, she gave a worried sigh, then locked the money in a tin box and put the box in a floor-safe.

Waco, who'd learned to walk Indian-quiet while scouting for the cavalry, descended the stairs soundlessly and crossed to the door.

The woman was so absorbed in her book-keeping she didn't hear him — until he opened the front door causing the little bell to tinkle. Startled, she whirled around with a gasp and became embarrassed as she saw him looking at her from the doorway.

'I'm awfully sorry,' she said in a cultured Bostonian voice. 'I didn't mean to ignore you. My mind was a million miles away and . . . '

'It's okay,' Waco said. 'It was my fault. I should've said something, but I didn't want to disturb you.'

'That's very thoughtful of you . . . '
The woman smiled and extended her
hand to him. 'I'm Mrs. Lockhart.
Georgina Lockhart — though most
everyone calls me Georgie.'

'Ma'am.' Waco shook her slim firm
hand and looked her over. He was
attracted by what he saw: a pretty face
that was both refined and farm-fresh,
and dark, luminous eyes filled with
warmth and compassion. She also had
a slight overbite that made her full lips
desirably kissable and in contrast, a shy
almost vulnerable demeanor that made
men like Waco want to protect her.

'Do I have something on my nose?'
she asked, smiling.

''Scuse me?'

'My nose . . . is there a smudge on
it?'

'No. Why?'

'I wondered, since you were staring
so hard.'

'S-Sorry. I didn't realize . . . I
mean . . . ' Waco gulped then added:
'Reckon you must be the owner of this

boarding house?'

'No, the bank owns it. But I'm working towards changing that. And you must have just checked in, Mr . . . uh' — she glanced at the register — 'McAllum.'

'A short while ago, yeah.'

'Dear me, I knew it,' Georgie said. 'I don't know why but guests always seem to register when I've stepped away from the desk for a few minutes. This time I was only in the kitchen long enough to heat up supper for my daughter — '

'Danny, right?'

'Yes.' Georgie smiled wearily, as if grudgingly resigned to her child's quirky behavior. 'Bet she warned you not to call her Daniella, didn't she?'

'Yep. She also told me not to say anything nice about the way she looked — which was pretty as springtime.'

'That's the problem.'

'I don't understand, ma'am.'

'Neither do I. At her age all I ever wanted was to look pretty and to wear beautiful dresses. But Daniella . . . '

Georgie paused and shook her head, puzzled, before adding: 'The strange thing is, Mr. McAllum, she used to be just like any other little girl.'

'What made her change? Do you know?'

'Nothing I can point to, no. It started — or at least became evident to me — around the same time her stepfather rode off and I used to blame him for it. But now, well, to be perfectly honest, I think that was just wishful thinking on my part.'

Waco hesitated, not sure if he should intrude any further. But the woman seemed so friendly, so unpretentious that he heard himself say: 'Well, it ain't none of my business of course, but what's your daughter's call on it?'

'That's the problem. Daniella refuses to discuss it with me. I've tried everything I know to get it out of her but she won't open up . . . so I guess I'll never know for sure.' Georgie sighed ruefully. 'All I do know is, nowadays she spends her entire time doing everything she can to act like and look like a boy.' She broke off, embarrassed, and then added: 'Please forgive me, Mr. McAllum. I have no right to burden you with my personal problems. It's just that — well, truthfully, I'm at my wits' end and . . . ' Her voice trailed off.

'It ain't no burden, ma'am. I like young'uns; 'specially young'uns with fire in their bellies, like your daughter.'

'Is that so?' Georgie gave an ironic laugh. 'Then you'd surely love my stepson. Mason would sooner split kindling than say a kind word to anyone.'

'Mason?' Waco wondered why the name sounded familiar. Then, as it came to him: ''Mean the boy over at the livery stable?'

'Yes. Why? Have you already run into him?'

Waco smiled wryly. 'Could say that.'

'Oh, dear, was he awfully rude to you?'

'Let's say he preferred my horse to me.'

'I'm sure he did, Mr. McAllum. But please, don't take it personally. Mason's always had this strange affinity for horses. Even when we lived in St. Louis, any time he was missing, I always knew where to find him. He'd be hanging around the local stables.'

Waco smiled. 'In that case, I reckon you're just going to have to accept the fact that you got two very unusual young'uns, Mrs. Lockhart.'

'I'm afraid there's no denying that,' she agreed.

Waco started to leave then paused, said: 'I've already poked my nose in your business too far, ma'am, but if you'll allow me one more question . . .'

'Of course.'

'The old man at the livery — he said some no-account fella named McCutcheon was Mason's pa — '

'He is . . . was . . .'

'Then?'

'Oh, you mean . . . why Lockhart?' She shrugged, resigned but not defeated. 'That was the surname of my first husband — Daniella's father. We lived in Boston at the time. But not long after Daniella was born, we moved to St. Louis where Ian — that was his name, Ian — caught pneumonia and . . . tragically passed away . . . ' She paused, as if the memory of her late husband was too painful for her to continue. Then, catching herself, she reddened and, slightly flustered, said: 'I'm sorry. Where was I?'

'You were about to tell me why you changed your name back to Lockhart,' Waco reminded.

'O-Oh, yes, of course. Well . . . I . . . uhm . . . when I eventually met and married Judd McCutcheon, naturally I took on his name. But later, not long after we settled here in Santa Rosa, he . . . abandoned us, so I decided to go back to Lockhart . . . hoping, I suppose, to erase that dreadful mistake from my mind.'

Waco studied the slim, wholesomely pretty woman looking at him from behind the front desk. Sensing her embarrassment for making such a mistake, he felt a need to say: 'Well, if you don't mind me saying so, ma'am, this McCutcheon fella, he must've been one big damn fool.' Tipping his hat, Waco reopened the door, making the tiny bell tinkle, and stepped out into the night.

Georgie looked after him for several moments, mind churning, and then without realizing that she was thinking aloud, said: 'You don't know it, Mr. McAllum, but that's the nicest thing anyone has said to me since dear Ian died.'

4

'Momma!' Danny's voice bellowed out through the open door behind the front desk. 'Better hurry. Supper's getting cold!'

'Coming, dear.' Georgie dragged her gaze from the door and entered the parlor.

It was a small, cozy room filled with delicate porcelain antiques that were older than Santa Rosa. Chintz floral curtains and elegant mahogany furniture that had been custom-made in Boston looked equally out of place. Once so highly polished Georgie could see her reflection in it, the beautiful furniture had gotten scratched during the train ride from Boston to St. Louis, then even more scratched and chipped during the wagon journey from St. Louis to New Mexico and now looked as shabby as the curtains.

Georgie joined her daughter at the table, which was covered by a white tablecloth. Made of fine Irish linen, it too had once been beautiful, but now due to too many washings and ironings it had turned yellow and shiny. At first the ruination of her treasured possessions had driven Georgie to despair. But she was too proud to quit or complain. She'd also loved her first husband and refused to leave him, despite her family's constant entreaties to come home. Instead she forced herself to adapt to her new surroundings. It hadn't been easy but gradually, over time, she'd learned to live with her reversal of fortunes and also the disastrous marriage to McCutcheon.

Now, removing her napkin from its hand-carved, yellowing ivory holder, she closed her eyes and said grace for both of them before ladling out servings of hot stew from a bowl on the table. 'You forgot the bread, dear.'

'Wasn't none to forget.'

'You mean we've already eaten it all?'

'Uh-huh.'

'Oh, then write a note for me, would you please, sweetheart, reminding me to bake some more tomorrow.'

Danny made a face. 'Couldn't you buy it from the baker instead, ma? His bread tastes so much better than yours.'

Georgie smiled, ruefully amused by her daughter's bluntness. 'Thank you, dear. But next time don't bother to spare my feelings. Just tell me straight out how you feel.'

'I just did,' grumbled Danny. 'I mean it ain't my fault if you can't even bake bread.'

'No, it isn't,' Georgie admitted. 'And you're quite right about which bread tastes best. But the baker's bread also costs more and right now I'm trying to save every cent I can to pay off the mortgage. That way, we'll never have to worry about being evicted.'

'I'm not worried,' her daughter said. 'I just wish you'd learn how to bake.'

'Me, too,' Georgie said, adding: 'Sweetheart, I know I haven't gotten the hang of baking yet, but I'll get better. I promise.'

'That's what you said 'bout your cooking, remember?'

'Yes, I know . . . ' Georgie gave a guilty little laugh. 'And hopefully I'll improve at that too. After all, like your father always said: practice makes perfect.'

'It's going to take a' awful lot of practice,' Danny muttered darkly.

Stung, Georgie said: 'That may be so. But what you must try to understand, dear, is when I was growing up in Boston I wasn't taught how to bake or cook. Mama assumed I wouldn't have any need for it. We had a chef and servants and she expected me to marry someone equally wealthy and well-positioned — '

'Yeah, yeah, yeah,' Danny grumbled. 'So you've told me a hundred times, ma.'

'Y-Yes, I'm sure I have. I'm sorry, dearest. I don't mean to be a bore. It's just that living like this has been such a cultural shock for me, especially since your beloved father passed . . . ' Her sad voice trailed off, and for several awkward moments neither spoke nor looked at each other. Then Georgie pressed her hand fondly over her daughter's, saying: 'I promise I'll try harder, Daniella. And I *will* get better. Really I will. But it won't happen overnight . . . and meanwhile I need you to be patient with me.'

Danny shrugged, 'All right, ma, I'll try,' and went on eating.

'And please, dear, do stop calling me ma. You know I hate that word, Daniella.'

'Yes, *mother*. I'm sorry, *mother*. I'll try to remember better next time, *mother*.'

'Now you quit that,' Georgie snapped. 'It's not in the least bit funny.'

'Neither's you calling me Daniella. You know I hate that name worse'n you hate ma.'

'That's nonsense! It's a delightful

name . . . so elegant and refined. And when you're not pretending to be a boy or an urchin from the streets, it suits you perfectly.'

'Baloney,' Danny scoffed. 'It's a sissy name and you know it.'

'I know nothing of the sort. What's more, I don't want you telling guests that your name is Danny. When they find out it isn't, I'm sure they must wonder what's wrong with you. They might even think you're backward and that could reflect badly on us and this boarding house. Is that clear?'

No answer.

'I said is that — ? Look at me when I'm talking to you, young lady,' Georgie insisted when her daughter turned away.

Danny sullenly obeyed. 'Happy?'

'Now you're being rude, and I won't stand for that.'

Danny picked up her spoon and began eating.

'Apologize, please.'

'Sorry.'

'Thank you.'

Her mother started eating. There was a long icy silence. Then:

'Pa didn't mind it when I called him pa,' Danny grumbled.

'Your father never minded *anything* you did,' Georgie replied. 'That's why you're so spoiled.'

5

Waco crossed Main Street and entered *La Rosarita*. It was crowded and noisy inside the popular cantina and the men drinking at the bar were too busy flirting with a large, big-breasted redheaded waitress to notice Waco. He pushed past them and found a table in back. It was still covered with the prior customers' dirty dishes but it faced the door, enabling him to see everyone who entered, so he pushed the dishes aside and sat.

The waitress took her own sweet time but finally sauntered over and asked Waco what he wanted to drink.

'A tall one that's not all froth,' he said. 'And whatever's cooking on the stove.'

'My, my, ain't you the trusting one.' She smiled invitingly at Waco. When he didn't respond, she turned sour and said tartly: 'Beans and tortillas suit you?'

Waco nodded and lit the hand-rolled he'd taken from behind his ear. 'Got any steak to go with that?'

'Depends how particular you are.'

'Meaning?'

'This morning the cook shot a coyote nosing around the trash.'

Waco didn't even smile at her joke. 'Burn it good. I hate meat that's still kicking.'

'I feel the same way about my men,' the waitress said.

'Then you don't have to worry 'bout me.'

'Too bad. I was just beginning to consider my options.' The waitress gathered up the dirty dishes and waltzed off.

* * *

Waco ate his supper slowly, enjoying every bite, pausing occasionally to quench his thirst with a long gulp of beer.

During the meal he noticed a tall, big-shouldered man with a gray mustache and a belly bulging over his belt-buckle, enter. He joked briefly with the waitress, who fawned over him in an effort to keep on his good side, then sat at a table facing Waco. He lit a cheroot and blew a smoke ring, lazily stretched out his long legs and surveyed the room.

Something about the man seemed vaguely familiar to Waco. Without being obvious, he sized him up. Pushing fifty, the man seemed overly impressed with himself. He also exuded a smug indifference, as if he was immune to criticism. In Waco's world that generally meant one of two things: he was fast with a gun or protected by someone rich and powerful. Wondering who he was and what he did, Waco got his answer when the man opened his jacket and clasped his hands across his belly.

It was then Waco noticed the sheriff's star glinting on his shirt.

Instantly Waco's mind flashed back to

the lynching. Though at the time he hadn't seen the sheriff's face, his size and paunch looked familiar, as did the star. Waco sensed he was looking at one of the men responsible for hanging his brother.

Forcing himself not to react, Waco lowered his eyes and continued eating. But he was now too tense to enjoy his food. He had to know for sure if this was one of the lynch mob and he had to know now. Quickly finishing his meal, he left money for the bill and a tip for the waitress and got to his feet. Hitching up his gun-belt, he started for the door. He had to pass the sheriff on the way out and the lawman, out of force of habit, raised his eyes to look Waco over.

For a moment Waco wondered if his recently-grown mustache and three weeks' stubble were enough of a disguise to prevent the sheriff from recognizing him. He surreptitiously removed the safety strap from the hammer of his gun in case it wasn't.

But he needn't have worried. Forbes showed no sign of remembering who he was and Waco decided to press his luck. He boldly met the lawman's inquiring gaze and stopped beside the table. ''Evening, sheriff.'

Sheriff Lonnie Forbes nodded his respects but didn't say anything.

'Was wondering if maybe you could help me out?'

'If I can, sure.'

'What trail do I take to get to the Double S ranch?'

'What's your business with Mr. Stadtlander?'

'Personal.'

'You'll have to do better than that.'

'Why? Are his whereabouts a secret?'

'No.'

'Then why you prodding me so hard?'

''Cause it's my job.' Forbes indicated the star on his shirt. 'See this? It gives me the right to prod strangers as much as I want.'

Waco shrugged. 'Well, if you must

47

know, sheriff, I'm looking for work.'

'Then I can save you a ride, mister. Last time I spoke to Mr. Stadtlander's foreman, Jason Prince, he said he didn't need any more hands.'

'Maybe things have changed since then.'

'I doubt it.'

'Well, think I'll ride out there anyway.'

'Why for would you want to do that?'

Instantly Waco froze. The last person he'd heard say 'why for' was the big paunchy man who'd been part of the lynch mob. Now he knew for certain that he was looking at one of his brother's murderers.

He immediately wanted to kill him and had to fight like hell not to draw his Colt.

Sheriff Forbes' voice interrupted Waco's thoughts. 'I asked you a question, mister.'

'S-Sorry. What was it?'

'I asked you why for you'd want to ride out to Mr. Stadtlander's place when I told you there wasn't no work to be had?'

Waco shrugged. 'What've I got to lose? Worst this Prince fella can say is no, right? And who knows, maybe one of the hands has quit since you two last talked, and then I have me a job I sorely need.'

Sheriff Forbes shrugged. 'Suit yourself, mister.'

Waco started to walk away, then turned and said: 'You're Lonnie Forbes, right?'

The sheriff squinted at Waco, trying to place him. He looked familiar and yet . . .

'It's all right,' Waco lied. 'We ain't never met. A fella I know told me about you.'

'This fella — he got a handle?'

'Rawlins. Latigo Rawlins.'

The sheriff tried not to react, failed, and said quickly: 'Y-You a bounty hunter, too?'

'Wrangler.'

The sheriff scoffed. 'With a pegged

rig and a fancy Merwin Hulbert revolver?'

'I keep my holster tied down,' Waco said, ''cause I don't like it flapping against my leg when I walk. As for the gun, M and H has been around almost as long as Colt, so there ain't nothing fancy or special about it.'

'First one I ever seen,' Sheriff Forbes said.

'But even if it *was* special,' Waco continued as if the lawman hadn't spoken, 'that don't make me a bounty hunter or a gunslinger for hire, like you're thinking. Truth is Lat and me both hail from the Brazos River country and one time over a beer he told me that he'd worked for the Double S and that Mr. Stadtlander was always looking for good hands. And that's the pure and only reason that brought me here.'

The sheriff absorbed Waco's words, decided he might be telling the truth and softened his attitude. 'Okay, son, I ain't fully convinced but I'll go along with you. As for Mr. Stadtlander, I'm heading out to the Double S in the morning. If you ain't allergic to company, be at my office 'round eight. You can ride with me.'

'Much obliged to you. Maybe you could even put in a good word for me?' Waco said. 'I mean coming from you, the sheriff, it might make all the difference.'

Sheriff Forbes eyed him shrewdly. 'You buttering me up, son?'

'Not intentionally,' replied Waco. 'But I reckon it could sound that way.'

'Well, 'least you ain't denying it. Tell you what. I'll think on it. Let you know in the morning.'

'Thanks. So long.' Waco respectfully tipped his hat and left.

The sheriff stared after him, still trying to figure out why he looked familiar.

'You know that cowboy?' he asked the waitress when she brought him his meal.

'Uh-uh. But I'd sure like to.'

'What were you two talking about

51

when I came in?'

'Nothing special. Why?'

'Did he tell you anything I should know about?'

'Like, what?'

'Where he was from? What brought him to Santa Rosa? If he was looking for someone in particular?'

'Nope. Nothing like that. We just flirted. You know? Like customers and waitresses always do.' She started away then stopped, looked back at the sheriff, said: 'Come to think of it, he did say one thing.'

Hooked, Sheriff Forbes eagerly leaned forward. 'What was that?'

'Said I was the best waitress he'd ever met and I deserved bigger tips than what you been leaving.' Chuckling, she hurried into the kitchen before the sheriff could stop her.

6

Once outside on the boardwalk, Waco stopped and tried to pull himself together. He looked at his gun-hand and by the light of a street lamp saw it was shaking. He had the greatest urge to go back into the cantina and blow the sheriff's head off. But he fought it down. He knew at the moment he couldn't prove Forbes was the same sheriff who'd watched while he and his brother were hung, and to force the issue now would not only prove futile but might damage any future chance he had of bringing the corrupt lawman to justice. So instead, he forced himself to calm down and returned to the rooming house.

The front door was locked. Waco used the key that Danny had given him and quietly climbed the dark stairs to his room. The door was partly open and through the crack Waco could see a kerosene lamp burning on the table. Wondering who the intruder was, he drew his gun, stood back from the line of fire and slowly toed the door fully open.

Sitting in a chair facing the door was a short, wiry man with curly yellow hair and a boyishly handsome face that masked a ruthless killer. He wore an expensive custom-made tan western-style suit, black string tie, hand-tooled boots and a spotless pearl-gray Stetson. Holstered on his hips were two ivory-handled, nickel-plated Colt .44s and Waco's sharp eye noticed a bulge under the man's jacket indicating he was carrying a belly gun.

But it wasn't his guns or his stylish clothes that people first noticed: it was his eyes. Like Waco's, they were unique. Amber-colored, they peered out from under long sandy lashes, mercilessly cold and constantly on the move, wary of everything and everyone as if expecting death to strike at any moment.

Waco, on seeing him, relaxed, holstered his six-gun and shook his head chidingly at the little bounty hunter. 'I should've known,' he said, entering and closing the door. 'Only you would have the gall to leave the door open, advertising you were in here, ready to gun someone down.'

'Why shouldn't I?' the man said matter-of-factly. 'I can slap leather fast enough to kill anyone, whether they've jerked their iron or not.'

'No argument there.' Waco grinned and offered his hand to the dapper little gunman. 'How the hell are you, Lat?'

'Couldn't be better,' Latigo Rawlins said, shaking hands. 'You?'

'Middling, thanks.'

'What brings you to Santa Rosa, *amigo*?'

'I'm looking for a killer or killers.'

Latigo's eyebrows arched with surprise and curiosity. 'Anybody I know?'

'Still working on that. But everything

points to Stillman J. Stadtlander — or someone who works for him.'

'Has to be the latter,' Latigo said.

'What makes you so sure?'

'Like I told you, I once hired my gun out to Stadtlander. Got to know his ways. He always pays to have his dirty work done. Not that he ain't capable of killing someone. It's just that he's too smart to risk losing everything for the satisfaction of pulling the trigger. You follow?'

Waco chewed on that for a moment before accepting the bounty hunter's word.

'Knowing you,' Latigo continued, 'you must've been prodded pretty hard to set out to kill someone. What happened?'

Waco sighed and sat on the edge of the bed.

'Before I answer that, Lat, where you been hiding of late? Not around here, that's for sure. I sent you two wires and you never answered either of them.'

'That's 'cause I was in Chihuahua.'

Waco frowned, surprised. 'Someone must've had a mighty big price on his head for you to cross the border.'

'This was pleasure, not business. I was with Gabe Moonlight, chasing the rabbit and trying to drink Palomas dry.'

'How'd that work out?'

'Well, Gabe and me, we done our best. But in the end we had to admit that cantinas can buy tequila faster than we can drink it.'

'Well, 'least you were doing something constructive.'

Latigo chuckled, his boyish grin making him look even younger and more innocent.

'How come you ain't still there?' Waco asked.

'Survival, *amigo*.'

'His or yourn?'

'Mine. Hell, another week with Gabe and I would've been feet up. Whooee, the way that man consumes liquor you'd swear he had a hollow leg.'

'I'll take your word for it,' Waco said. 'I only met Gabe once and that was before the law chased him into Mexico for being a horse thief — '

'*Accused* of being a horse thief,' Latigo corrected. 'Big difference, *amigo*.'

'Gabe was railroaded?'

'Yeah, by Stadtlander.'

'Why?'

'It's a long story.'

'Tell me the cheap-seats version.'

Latigo collected his thoughts, said: 'Some years back Gabe won this blooded, all-black Morgan stallion, Brandy, with aces and eights.'

'Dead man's hand?'

'Unlucky for Wild Bill Hickok, lucky for Gabe. Anyways, Stadtlander offered Gabe a lot of money for the stallion but Gabe refused to sell it. Stadtlander ain't used to being told no, and warned Gabe that he'd be sorry for defying him. Gabe ignored the warning, figuring that Stadtlander was bluffing, and rode off. But Stadtlander wouldn't let it go. He come right out and accused Gabe of stealing Brandy from him. No one took him seriously at first — until he pressed charges and bribed a judge to make them legal.'

''Be damned.'

'Once it was official that Gabe was a horse thief, Stadlander then ordered his pet skunk to go hunt him down and stretch his neck.'

'That'd be Sheriff Forbes you're talking about?'

Latigo nodded, removed his Stetson and ran his fingers through his blond curls. 'The bastard hides in Stadlander's pocket most of the time. That way Stillman can bring him out whenever he needs the law to enforce one of his lies or land-grabbing schemes.'

'Doesn't sound like a man who'd be welcome at the Pearly Gates.'

'Forget heaven,' Latigo scoffed. 'Hell, even the devil hisself would have second thoughts about joining forces with Stadlander.'

'But it didn't stop you.'

'Meaning?'

'Even though you knew all about

Stadlander, you still went to work for him.'

'So?'

'Was wondering how you justified that?'

'Money's money, *amigo*, no matter who's giving it to you.'

'Got to bury your conscience pretty deep to truly believe that.'

'I don't got to bury nothing. Hell's fire, it ain't my job to decide who's guilty and who ain't. I'm paid just to bring law-breakers in.'

'Dead or alive?'

Latigo shrugged. 'That's up to them — though I ain't denying that dead makes it easier all around.' Pausing, he licked his lips and said: 'I hate to change the subject, but I could sorely use two fingers about now. Got a bottle hid 'round here somewhere, do you?'

'Here, try this.' Waco dug a flask from his pocket and tossed it to Latigo.

'*Gracias.*'

'Kill it,' Waco said as Latigo took a swig and started to return the flask. 'I need to have my brains straight while I'm trying to track down the men who hung Chris.'

Latigo stopped in mid-swallow, eyes popping. 'Y-You're brother's dead?'

Waco nodded regretfully.

'When?'

'A while back now.'

'How? I mean what for?'

'He and a pal were supposedly caught red-handed altering brands on rustled beef.'

'That don't sound like Chris.'

'That's what I tried to tell them. But they strung him up anyways.'

'They?'

'Stadtlander's foreman, Jason Prince and a bunch of Double S riders.'

Latigo frowned. 'That don't sound like Jason, either. He's tough, maybe tougher than his brother Jim who works for Major Devlin. But Jason's fair. He'd accept a hanging but he'd never lynch nobody.'

'Tell Chris that,' Waco said grimly. 'And me too, while you're at it.'

'Meaning?'

Waco unbuttoned the collar of his shirt, revealing an ugly rope burn circling his neck.

'Holy Jesus,' Latigo breathed. 'They tried to hang you, too?'

'They did hang me. I'd be as dead as my brother if the rope hadn't broke.'

'How come they didn't string you up again?'

'They'd ridden off by then or they would've.' Waco re-buttoned his collar.

Latigo whistled softly. 'God*damn*,' he said. 'Reckon there's no disputing a scar like that.'

'Yet you still ain't convinced. I can hear it in your voice.'

Latigo shrugged. 'Like I said, it's not like Jason to lynch someone. You *are* sure it was him, right?'

'Pretty sure. He and his men wore hoods, but I recognized that gravelly voice of his from back when we used to ride herd together for the Lazy J. It was definitely Jason all right. And that means it was Double S boys who were helping him, which also means that Stadtlander's somehow tied into it, too.'

'Anyone else involved?'

Waco didn't answer but his expression turned grim.

'Well?'

Waco hesitated then said: 'I'll tell you who it is when I can prove it.'

'Is he someone I know?'

'If it's who I think it is, yeah.'

'Is he from around here?'

'No, Mesilla. But he lives and works here now.'

Latigo frowned. 'Sure you don't want to tell me who he is?'

'You'll know soon enough,' Waco said grimly, 'if I'm right about him.'

Latigo accepted that, thought a moment, said: 'How you going to prove it?'

'I ain't sure yet. But if and when I do, it's going to be a real pleasure killing him.'

'Amen to that.' Latigo let his thoughts stew for a minute before adding: 'Well, one thing's for sure: that rope burn on your neck proves *someone* hanged you. But since you never saw any faces, just heard voices, I got to tell you, *amigo,* it ain't going to be easy proving who that someone is or was. You follow?'

'Then you still don't think it was Jason and the Double S boys?'

'Didn't say that. Hell, how would I know who it was? I wasn't there. Maybe it was, maybe it wasn't. I'd believe you either way. But dammit, something in my gut tells me that there's definitely more to this than meets the eye.'

'I agree,' Waco said. 'That's why I'm here: to find out what that 'more' is and then deal with it accordingly.'

Latigo frowned, concerned. 'You *do* know who you're going up against, right?'

'I know Stadtlander's the most powerful cattleman in this territory, if that's what you mean.'

'Exactly.' Latigo fell silent, mind churning. Then coming to a decision, he rose and put his hat on, flicked his cigarette out the window and confronted Waco. 'You're going to need help, *amigo*. And plenty of it.'

'I know. But this ain't your fight, so — '

'I'm making it mine. Chris was a good kid. Mite wild, maybe, but deep down good. If some bastard lynched him, like you say, I want to know who and why, too.'

'Thanks. 'Preciate that.'

'But that don't alter the fact that we're going to need more guns — men we can count on when the going gets rough. And believe me, it *will* get rough!'

'Got someone in mind?'

'Two 'someones.' C'mon.' Latigo hitched up his gun-belt and started for the door. 'Let's make some dust.'

7

'Wait, hold up,' Waco said as they reached the street outside the boarding house. 'Where we headed?'

'To the telegraph office. I want to send a wire.'

'Mite late in the day for that. The office is most likely closed.'

'So we'll get the station agent to open it for us.'

'He's going to love that.'

'He won't care,' Latigo said. 'Lew Swain's a miserable tightwad. Wave a few greenbacks under his nose and there ain't nothing he wouldn't do. You follow?'

They continued on along Main Street, the little yellow-and-brown station-house now visible ahead. A warm wind came sweeping up from the border. Both men grimaced as it filled their noses with the stench of the cattle pens lining the railroad tracks.

'Who you sending a wire to?' Waco asked as they neared the station.

'Marshal Macahan in El Paso. I want him to get hold of Drifter for me.'

'Who?'

'Drifter. You don't know him?'

'Uh-uh.'

'Quint Longley's his real name,' Latigo explained, 'but everyone calls him Drifter on 'count of the fact that when he was young, he never stayed in one place for long.'

'Why him?'

'He can handle a gun and has no love for Stadtlander. He's also pals with Macahan.'

'Who I don't know either,' Waco said. 'Though I did get to *enjoy* his hospitality one night when I was in El Paso a few years back.'

Latigo chuckled. 'What'd he haul your ass in for?'

'Getting skunked on cactus wine laced with peyote.'

'Jesus! Serves you right, *amigo*. Next

time stick to plain tequila.'

'Don't worry. There won't be no next time. I've learned my lesson. But back to Macahan and Drifter,' Waco added, 'how are lawmen going to help my cause?'

'Drifter ain't a lawman.'

'But Macahan is. And he'll want to do things strictly legal, which works against me. Hell, it's just my word against a bunch of men wearing hoods. Any judge in his right mind would toss me out of the courtroom 'fore I got a chance to open my mouth.'

'Not if you can prove who those men were.'

'How do I do that? And even if by some miracle I *did* prove it was Jason and the Double S riders, no jury in Santa Rosa would ever convict them. They'd be too scared of reprisals.'

'Not if the jurors were more afraid of us than Stadtlander.'

'How's that going to happen? You going to threaten to shoot 'em?'

'You're joking, but I ain't.'

Waco stared at Latigo as if he was loco. 'You can't be serious?'

Latigo shrugged. 'Fight fire with fire, as my old man used to say.'

'And it got him a stretch in Yuma penitentiary. Which is where we'll end up if we're caught tampering with a jury.'

'We won't *get* caught, *amigo*. Anyways, it won't ever come to that. Once the jurors know they got to answer to me and you and maybe Drifter and Gabe, too — hell, they'll be begging to side with us.'

Waco sighed, unable to believe what he was getting into. 'Okay, just for argument's sake say I go along with you. Before we can persuade Gabe and this Drifter fella to join us, we first got to find 'em — and fast.'

'No sweat. Gabe's either sobering up in Palomas or holed up at the Bjorkman spread. So there'll be no problem roping him. As for Drifter, he's settled down now. He owns a horse ranch with his daughter, Emily, just outside El

Paso. Macahan will know how to reach him. Then Drifter can catch the morning train up here.'

'Okay,' Waco admitted, 'so it ain't impossible. But you're forgetting one important fact: why would either of them risk their neck for me? Gabe's only met me once and Drifter, he don't even know who I am.'

'Leave Gabe to me,' Latigo said. 'Once he's heard your story and knows that Stadtlander's involved, he'll gladly throw in with us.'

'And Drifter?'

'I got that covered too. I'll sign Gabe's name to the wire. If Drifter thinks Gabe's the one asking him for help, how can he say no?'

'In other words, lie to him?'

'Just for starters, yeah.'

'And when he gets here and finds out the truth,' Waco said, 'what's to stop him from being so pissed off he shoots both of us?'

'Me,' Latigo drawled, patting his guns. 'No matter how angry Drifter is, he ain't stupid enough to draw on me. He knows he'd be a candidate for a pine box. Relax,' he added as Waco looked dubious. 'I know what I'm doing, *amigo*.'

8

The Bjorkman spread was a short ride southwest from Santa Rosa. Once barely large enough to support a few cattle, horses and hogs, lately it had grown significantly thanks to a considerable fortune that Ingrid Bjorkman had inherited. She'd not been expecting any inheritance and was happily shocked when six months ago a Danish lawyer contacted her, explaining that her great uncle in Odense had died and left his entire estate to her. Once over her surprise, Ingrid waited for the money to clear probate court then purchased all the range surrounding her property, with intentions of stocking it with prime cattle.

Previously, the land had belonged to her neighbors, who'd settled there long before Ingrid and her late husband, Sven, arrived from Odense. In those early days the southwest had been brutal to settlers. For years they'd fought marauding Apaches and Comanches, survived prolonged droughts and repeated outbreaks of blackwater fever, all the while struggling to make ends meet. Then, as if life wasn't already hard enough, they were confronted by a new menace: veiled threats by Stillman J. Stadtlander, who needed their land to feed his ever-increasing herd but was unwilling to pay more than a pittance for it.

Powerful and ruthless, he preferred to have his gunmen terrorize the families, hoping that sooner or later they'd grow tired of their cabins being burned, their children scared, their livestock stampeded and their vegetable gardens destroyed and beg him to buy their property. But he had underestimated them. The sod-busters, as he called them, proved tougher than he'd expected, stubbornly refusing to sell despite his constant pressure.

But even they could only survive so long. A few months ago, the more desperate families had begun to talk about leaving and homesteading elsewhere, like in Arizona or California. Because of this, they were only too happy to accept Ingrid's unexpected but more-than-fair prices for their spreads and quickly sold their ranches and farms to her.

Once she'd bought the land, Ingrid made it known in Santa Rosa that she was looking for a responsible, experienced foreman to not only ramrod her ever-expanding ranch but to help her buy the best purebred cattle possible to stock her herd. Several men applied for the job, but none of them impressed Ingrid and she was still looking for the right man.

'Momma!' It was her daughter, Raven, calling to her from the corral where she was rope-training an unbroken colt. 'Riders a-coming.'

Ingrid appeared in the doorway of their cabin, drying her hands on a dish-towel. 'Can you make out who they are, sweetheart?'

'Just one of 'em,' Raven said. A precocious tomboy of fourteen, she had short crow-black hair and straight-cut bangs that made her big dark eyes seemed even larger. A life outdoors had tanned her skin as brown as tobacco, while her slim lithe body looked at home in torn jeans and a sun-faded blue shirt. 'It's that bounty hunter friend of Gabe's, Mr. Rawlins.'

'Latigo?' Ingrid said, surprised. 'I thought he was in Mexico with Gabriel.'

'Maybe he was,' her daughter said. 'But not now he ain't.'

'Isn't,' corrected Ingrid. She was slim and fair-skinned, with sky-blue eyes and sun-streaked tawny hair and, like most Norwegians, hard to rattle. 'My good-ness, child, when are you going to learn to speak correctly?'

Raven scowled defiantly. 'Momma, don't you ever listen to me?'

'What do you mean?'

'I already answered that question yesterday: *after* you and Gabe get hitched.'

Ingrid rolled her eyes. 'Now don't start harping on that again,' she chided. 'You know perfectly well why Gabriel and I can't get married — now or most likely ever.'

'That's hogwalla and you know it.'

Her mother, in no mood to argue, didn't respond.

'Being an outlaw didn't stop Jesse James from getting hitched.'

'Who?'

'Jesse James. Mr. Gustafson told me — '

'Whoa, wait a minute. What were you doing in his livery stable?'

'Playing checkers.'

Ingrid looked doubtfully at her daughter. 'When was this?'

'Last month, when we were in town and you were off buying supplies.'

'Oh.'

'Anyways, 'cording to Mr. Gustafson, right after the Civil War Jesse and his brother Frank started robbing banks and trains. They bungled a few robberies to start with, but once they got the hang of it and kept riding off with big payrolls, the head of the railroad got so angry he offered a big reward for them, dead or alive.'

'That doesn't sound particularly appealing.'

'Maybe not, Momma, but it proves my point.'

'Which is?'

'Being an outlaw didn't stop Jesse from marrying his sweetheart.'

'*Or* getting shot in the back for the reward money,' Ingrid reminded her, ' — *if* I recall correctly.'

'Mr. Gustafson said that only happened 'cause Jesse trusted the wrong man,' Raven said. 'Gabe would never do that.'

'Perhaps not,' her mother replied. 'But even so, what you're suggesting is hardly the recipe for a storybook marriage.'

'Never said it was. All I said was,

Jesse James wasn't killed 'cause he got married.'

Ingrid, tired of arguing, especially under a scorching sun, went back into the cabin to prepare coffee for her approaching visitors.

9

'Sorry to bust in on you like this,' Latigo said, after he'd introduced Ingrid to Waco. 'But I was hoping you could help us.'

'I haven't seen Gabe lately,' she said, 'if that's what you're going to ask me. As a matter of fact, I thought the two of you were still propping up bars in Palomas.'

'Nah. I sobered up a couple of weeks ago and rode back to Santa Rosa.'

'Then Gabe, I take it, is still in Palomas?'

'Last I heard, yeah.' Latigo turned to Waco. 'Since he ain't here, reckon we're going to have to ride across the border after all.'

'That's fine with me. You figure we can track him down by nightfall?'

'Depends on how much — ' About to say 'whoring around,' Latigo caught

79

himself in time and instead said: ' — fun Gabe's having.'

Not fooled, Ingrid scowled at Latigo, her tone hardening as she demanded: 'So, what fracas do you need him to bail you out of this time?'

'Hold on now, Ingrid,' he said indignantly. 'I ain't looking for Gabe, Waco is.'

'That's right,' admitted Waco. 'I'm the one you should be tongue-lashing, Mrs. Bjorkman, not Lat. And by the way, if you don't want your man to help us, ma'am, just say the word.'

Ingrid sighed wearily. 'If only it was that easy, Mr. McAllum. But with Gabe, nothing ever is. I'm not complaining, you understand? God knows, I knew exactly what I was getting into when we first started our relationship. So no one's at fault here except me. But . . . ' She paused and gazed into her coffee cup as if hoping to find answers there. When she didn't, she looked across the table at the men facing her. 'The truth is, Mr.

McAllum, as Lat will tell you, I never get involved in Gabe's affairs. He leads his life, I lead mine. He knows I love him and that there'll always be a home here for him, should he ever be pardoned, but that's as far as it goes between us.'

She sounded resigned but in no way bitter and both men respected her for it.

'Well,' Latigo said, rising, 'guess it's time we were making dust. Thanks for the coffee, Ingrid.'

'Yeah,' Waco said, rising. 'And for letting us water our horses, ma'am.'

'Anytime,' Ingrid said. She waited for them to leave then took their cups to the sink.

Moments later Latigo poked his head back in the doorway. 'Anything you want me to tell Gabe when I see him?'

Ingrid shook her head, smiled wistfully. 'He's already heard everything I've got to say, many times over.'

'Yeah,' Latigo agreed. 'Reckon he has

at that.' He politely tipped his hat and left.

Ingrid heard them mount up. She looked out the window in the direction of Mexico. Gabriel — *her* Gabriel — was out there somewhere and just the thought of him made her heart ache. Though strong-willed and accustomed to hardship and deprivation, there were times when even her determination wavered. During those times, she longed to be close to him, to feel his strong arms about her and his kisses on her lips. Now was one of those times and it took all her willpower not to round up her daughter, saddle two horses and accompany Latigo and Waco across the border.

But, as always, she controlled her emotions and instead went to the door. 'Lat',' she called out, 'can you spare a minute?'

'Sure.' Latigo reined up and rode back to her. 'What do you need?'

'I was wondering if you know anyone who's qualified to help me buy a prize bull and some cattle worth breeding him to — someone who'd be loyal and I could trust?'

'Then it's true?'

'What?'

'That you're rich and have been buying up the local spreads?'

'I wouldn't call myself rich exactly,' Ingrid replied. 'But yes, I have been buying up the land around me.'

'I'll be damned . . . ' Latigo shook his head in disbelief. 'Some men have all the luck.'

'If you mean Gabriel,' Ingrid said, irked, 'I'd remind you that he's got a price on his head for stealing his own horse — a horse Stadtlander claims is his — and because of that lie, he has a rope waiting for him on this side of the border. So I'd hardly call him lucky.'

'Could be worse, ma'am.'

'How?'

'He could be without you.'

'That's very flattering,' Ingrid said, blushing. 'But all the flattery in the world can't make up for the time

83

Gabriel and I have lost together, thanks to Stadtlander's lies!'

'True. But Stillman's a bitter old man who's on his last legs. And once he's dead, no one will think of Gabe as an outlaw. 'Least, not around here. Folks will just remember him for the good man he is and won't give a hoot if he stays with you or even marries you for that matter. You follow?'

Ingrid nodded. 'I only hope you're right. But for now, spending a few hours a month with the man you love — hours, I might add, that neither of us can fully enjoy for fear that a bushwhacker's bullet or a posse's rope could end it all — is hardly an ideal relationship.'

'Maybe not,' Latigo said, looking at her in a way that made her blush. 'But I'd take it in a heartbeat.' Before Ingrid could respond, he wheeled his horse around and spurred it in the direction of the border.

Surprised by Latigo's sudden departure, Waco tipped his hat to Ingrid and rode after him. But he'd only ridden a little ways when he reined up and came riding back to her. ''Bout the fella you're looking for, ma'am — the ramrod to help you start your own herd?'

'Yes, Mr. McAllum?'

'If you ain't in a rush to hire someone, Mrs. Bjorkman, I'm your man.'

'You?' Ingrid looked dubiously at Waco. 'I'm sorry, Mr. McAllum. But I need a foreman, not a gunman.'

'You got the wrong impression of me, ma'am. I'm no gunman. I been a wrangler and a cowhand all my life. If my kid brother hadn't been lynched, I wouldn't even be here. Believe me, I can break broomtails and handle a branding iron with the best of 'em.'

'I'm sure you can. But I need more than that. I need a man who's an expert on selective breeding.'

'Well, I ain't no expert,' Waco admitted, 'but I do know something about it. And I learn fast, ma'am. I been around cattle all my life. I've seen every kind of bull you can think of. I've also watched their offspring grow up to be everything from blue ribbon calves to bitter disappointments. And during that time I've learned one thing: there ain't no such thing as a sure thing. No one can guarantee you anything, not when it comes to offspring. And anyone who claims he can — well, he's a flat-out liar.'

'I see.'

'As for me, ma'am, all I can offer you is a fair day's work for fair wages. That and my honest opinion about cattle, selective breeding or anything else you ask me. If that fits in your plans, Mrs. Bjorkman, then, like I said before, I'm your man.'

'How about references?' Ingrid asked — and immediately wished she hadn't.

'I got them too,' Waco said, adding: 'Up until recently — 'fore my kid brother was lynched — I was the foreman of a big spread north of Laredo: the Running Bar-Z.'

'Really?' Ingrid said, eyes widening.

'You've heard of it then?'

'I have indeed.'

'If you wired the owner, Reed Ketchum, I'm sure he'd back up my words.'

Ingrid didn't respond right away. She looked at Waco, long and hard, as if trying to evaluate him. She didn't know why but for some reason she couldn't pinpoint, she trusted him. 'Very well,' she said finally. 'I'll take you at your word, Mr. McAllum. But . . . '

'Yes, ma'am?'

'I think it's only fair to warn you. I can't hold this job open for more than a week or two at most. So if you and Mr. Rawlins are planning to stay in Mexico any longer than that, I'll have to find someone else. Is that clear?'

'Perfectly, ma'am. But don't worry, Mrs. Bjorkman. I can't speak for Lat', but me — I'll be back long before then.' Tipping his hat, Waco turned his horse around and rode after Latigo . . . now a diminishing silhouette on the horizon.

10

It was dusk when they reached Palomas. Gabriel was not in any of his usual haunts, but after asking around Waco and Latigo eventually found him in a second-floor room in the rundown Hotel *Cielo*. Naked save for his boots, he had passed out in bed in the arms of the two prettiest whores in town — which, considering that Palomas was famous for its ugly whores, wasn't saying a hell of a lot.

'Jesus,' breathed Waco, appalled by Gabe's sotted condition. 'You reckon he's still alive?'

'One way to find out.' Latigo pinched Gabe's nose and with his other hand squeezed the outlaw's lips together, preventing him from breathing.

For a moment Gabe didn't respond. Then, eyes still closed, he fought for breath and clumsily knocked Latigo's hands away from his nose and mouth.

'Yep,' Latigo said as Gabe gulped in air. 'Sonofagun's alive all right. But by his looks, I wouldn't want to bet for how long.' Turning to the two half-breed whores, he growled: '*Vamos! Vamos! Comprende?*' he added when they didn't respond. 'Git!'

'B-But, *señor*,' one whore protested, 'Mr. Gabe, he owe us *mucho dinero*.'

Latigo drew one of his ivory-handled .44s, thumbed back the hammer and aimed the Colt at the whores. 'Money won't do you no good if you're both dead, now, will it?'

The two fleshy, naked Pima-Mexican whores panicked. Scrambling out of bed, they grabbed their clothes and fled.

'You and Mr. Colt sure do have a way with words,' Waco chuckled.

''Specially when they spell lead poisoning,' said Latigo. Going to the bed, he added: 'Now, grab this sorry sonofabuck's feet and help me carry him down the back stairs.'

'What about his things?'

'I'll come back for 'em.'

Outside, behind the seedy old hotel, was a trough filled with putrid water.

Waco took one look at it and turned as green as the slime coating the surface.

'M-Maybe we should find cleaner water?'

'Like hell,' Latigo said.

'But — '

'Don't you worry none about Gabe, *amigo*. If all the cheap firewater he's swallowed this past month ain't killed him, nothing will. Now, on three, okay? One, two . . . *three*!'

They dumped Gabe into the slimy water, both of them jumping back to avoid being splashed, and watched as he sank below the scummy surface.

'I'll go get his things,' Latigo said and hurried off before Waco could stop him.

* * *

A little later, when Latigo returned with Gabe's hat, clothes and gun-belt he found Waco nursing his jaw and Gabe, still naked save for his now-wet boots and covered in green slime, holding Waco's gun and raging at him from the other side of the trough.

'Y-You no-good, pig-puking bastard!' he roared at him. 'I'm going to blast your innards to hell!'

'Now there's gratitude for you,' Latigo said to Waco. 'We save the sonofagun from being robbed, maybe even killed by those whores and this is all the thanks we get!'

'I told you he wouldn't appreciate it,' Waco said, playing along. 'But you wouldn't listen. Said you knew him better than me . . . ' He paused then turned to Gabe, adding: 'Kept telling me how you were an understanding sort of gent and that when you knew the facts you'd not only thank us, but would buy us the finest steak in town. But I can see now he was wrong. You're a mean ornery cuss, just as I suspected. We should've let them whores gut you neck-to-gizzard and gone on about our own goddamn business.'

'He's right, Gabe,' Latigo added. 'If I knowed you was going to turn on us, I wouldn't stopped them whores from slitting your throat and stealing you blind!'

Gabe glared at them, unconvinced. 'You're lying, both of you . . . so quit blowing smoke up my ass. Them whores wouldn't have robbed me . . . much less killed me. Why would they? Hell, they'd be losing one of their best customers.'

'Have it your own way,' Latigo said. Then to Waco: 'Did you give that fat whore her knife back?'

'No, I tossed it out the window, like you told me.'

'What knife?' Gabe interrupted.

'Good,' Latigo said, ignoring Gabe. 'She was probably just funning with us, but you can never tell about whores. Some of 'em have a real mean streak and will cut you up just for the joy of it.'

'*What* knife?' Gabe repeated.

'Ain't that the truth?' Waco agreed. 'Hell, I know of one fella who was carved up by a whore and then, if that wasn't bad enough, she cooked his remains and stuffed tamales with 'em. Sold 'em by the dozen.'

'Doesn't surprise me,' Latigo said. 'Some of the tamales I've ate tasted like — '

Tired of being ignored, Gabe grabbed Latigo and Waco by the arm and spun them around so that they faced him. 'Answer me, goddammit! What knife are you two jokers talking about?'

'The one I thought the fat whore was going to use on you,' Waco replied. ''Course, I realize now I was imagining it. You, trusting her like you do, would have known better. You would've known she was just going to — to — ' He paused and looked questioningly at Latigo, who quickly said to Gabe: 'Shave you.'

'Exactly,' Waco continued. 'Shave you. 'Course, the fact that you wasn't lathered up, like in a barbershop, might've influenced me some. Still, I'm real ashamed of myself for not trusting her. *And* for throwing away her knife.'

'Maybe next time you see her, Waco,' Latigo suggested, 'you should give her a few pesos so she can buy a new pig-sticker.'

'Now that's a real good idea, *compadre*.'

Gabe, who'd been looking back and forth at the two men, still unsure whether or not to believe them, now said: 'You ain't joshing me? Maria, she really did have a knife?'

'Sure looked like a knife to me,' Waco said, stifling his amusement. 'I mean, I've seen my fair share of knives, so I know what a knife looks like, and, yep, this looked like a knife to me. But if you got any doubts — '

'No, no, I believe you,' Gabe said, convinced now. 'It's just . . . '

'Just what?'

'It don't figure.'

'What don't?'

'Maria — wanting to cut me up.' He frowned, mind churning, then said:

'Admittedly, I short-changed her a few pesos a few months back. Wasn't done intentional like, you understand, but she must've thought it was and figured on making me pay for it.'

'That's a whore for you,' Latigo said, fighting to keep a straight face. 'They can hold grudges longer than a goddamn elephant — '

'Yeah,' added Waco, 'and for the dumbest damn' reasons, too.'

Gabe nodded, the gun in his hand now hanging loosely at his side.

'Maybe you should put your pants on, *amigo*,' Latigo said, offering Gabe his clothes and gun-belt. 'Then go back to your hotel room and take a bath . . . wash that slime off you. You're starting to smell a tad ripe.'

'Good idea,' Gabe said. 'Reckon I'll do just that and afterwards, buy me some new duds . . . boots an' all.'

'First,' Waco said as casually as he could, 'how 'bout giving me back my iron?'

'W-What?' Gabe looked at Waco's

.44–40 revolver as if seeing it for the first time. 'Oh, sure. Here . . . ' He handed Waco the gun, adding: 'Sorry I took a poke at you. But, what the hell, taking a bath in scummy water like that can ferment any fella's brain.'

'Forget it,' Waco said, holstering his six-shooter. 'In your place I would've done the exact same thing.'

'Mighty white of you to say that,' Gabe said. He offered Waco his hand and the two men shook.

Latigo, trying to stifle his laughter, somehow kept a straight face as he said to Gabe: 'Maybe after you've washed up, the three of us can bend an elbow at *El Tecolote*?'

'On one condition,' Gabe said. 'Drinks are on me. No,' he added as they started to protest. 'I insist. I owe you both an apology anyways.'

'Fair enough,' Latigo said. 'See you at the bar in about an hour, okay?' Fighting not to laugh, he and Waco hurried off before Gabe had time to disagree.

11

El Tecolote was crowded and noisy as usual. The big stuffed owl, for which the popular cantina was named, stared down from the rafters, its big glass eyes focused on the mariachi players and the rowdy customers drinking at the bar. Suddenly it gave a series of loud, mechanical hoots. As if on cue, the grandfather clock that had originally belonged to the once-haughty-now-deceased Don Diego family chimed eight times. Immediately everyone turned, raised their glasses and proudly toasted the magnificent old clock. It was an age-old ritual that, like the clock, had become legendary. No one could remember when it started, just as no one could remember when the clock became the property of the cantina, but each year a new and even more preposterous tall tale surfaced and was immediately accepted as if it were true into local lore.

Gabe pushed in through the doors just as the last chime sounded. Bathed, shaved and wearing new boots, jeans and a gray denim shirt he looked almost human again, though his eyes were red-raw and his head still pounded from an ungodly hangover. Tall enough to see over everyone's head, he spotted Latigo and Waco drinking tequila shots at a corner table and made his way over to them.

He sank into a chair opposite them, groaned as his head spun and gently squeezed the bridge of his nose in an attempt to ease the pressure and clear up his blurred vision.

'Got just the remedy for that,' Latigo said. Grabbing the half-empty bottle of tequila, he filled an extra shot glass and set it, a salt shaker and a slice of lime in front of Gabe.

'Hair of the dog, *amigo*.'

Gabe started to say no, thought

better of it, 'Ah, what the hell,' sprinkled salt on the back of his hand, licked it and gulped down the tequila. He then sucked on the lime.

'*Te sientes mejor?*' Latigo asked him.

'Much better,' Gabe said. He poured himself another shot of tequila and repeated the whole process. Then leaning back in his chair, he studied his friends through steeple-shaped fingers. 'So why exactly are you here? And don't feed me any crap 'bout how you wanted to save my life, 'cause I ain't in the damn' mood for it.'

'Delightful soul, ain't he?' Latigo said, grinning at Waco. 'Go ahead,' he then added. 'You tell him, *amigo*. It's your story. But don't leave nothing out 'cause I want Gabe to get the whole picture 'fore he signs on.'

Waco quickly explained what had happened. Gabe listened without saying a word. But when Waco reached the part where his kid-brother Chris had been lynched by Stadtlander's foreman and the Double S riders, Gabe's expression turned thunderous and with a muttered curse, he gulped down another shot of tequila.

'So what do you think?' Latigo asked him when Waco was finished. 'You want in on this or not?'

'Reckon you already know the answer to that,' Gabe replied. Then to Waco: 'I'll help you all I can. But you ought to know right away that there's going to be plenty of gunplay. Stadtlander's got a heap of men riding for him and they're all more than handy with a gun. So if you know anyone else who'll join us, now's the time to round them up.'

'I don't,' said Waco. 'But Latigo thinks he can get Drifter to throw in with us — '

'Only thinks?' Gabe said hollowly.

'Truth is I'm pretty sure of it,' Latigo said. 'You know Clint. Nothing he likes better than a good fight, 'specially if the odds are against him. You follow?'

'Well, he should be right happy then,' Gabe said. ''Cause the way I figure it, they might go as high as ten to one.'

'On top of that,' Latigo continued doggedly, 'like you, Clint don't regard old man Stadtlander too favorably.'

'I'll second that,' Gabe said. 'Hopefully, that'll be enough to get him to agree — '

Suddenly, the raucous laughter going on around them stopped as everyone turned to watch two drunks getting into it at the bar. Before the fighting got out of hand one of the two barkeeps grabbed a club from under the bar and bounced it off the nearest drunk's head. He collapsed without a sound and lay in a heap on the sawdust-covered floor. The barkeep then threatened to hit the other drunk, who quickly backed away, hands raised in surrender, and stumbled out of the cantina.

The barkeep tucked the club away and returned to fixing drinks.

The other customers continued their conversations as if nothing had happened and within moments it was as noisy as ever.

Waco, who had been watching the action, now turned to Gabe and said: 'Look. I know this ain't an ideal situation and I wouldn't blame you if you changed your mind and rode out of here. In fact, in your boots I'd probably do just that and never look back.'

Gabe didn't say anything. He just eyed Latigo as if asking him 'what-the-hell-have-you-got-me-into?'

For a moment Waco felt for sure that the tall man was going to turn him down . . . which was why he was so surprised when Gabe suddenly laughed boisterously and slapped his knee.

'By Joshua!' he exclaimed. 'You're a man who lays it all on the line, ain't you?'

It was a statement more than a question and Waco remained silent.

'Well, my friend, I'm here to tell you that I'm a man who likes a man who shows you his cards and then dares you to beat him. Yessir, I surely do.'

'That mean you're in?' Latigo asked.

'Up to my bootstraps.'

'What'd I tell you, *amigo*?' Latigo said to Waco. 'I knew we could count on him.'

Waco grinned, relieved, and stuck out his hand to Gabe. 'Thanks.'

Gabe shook hands but before he could say anything, Latigo continued glibly: 'Now that you're with us, partner, I was wondering if maybe you could do us a favor?'

'Name it,' Gabe said.

'Would you wire Macahan and — '

'Ezra Macahan? Whoa, hold it right there. The marshal wouldn't help us. He's a strictly-by-the-book lawman. First thing he'd do is arrest me and toss my sorry ass in jail and then order the town fathers to start building a gallows.'

'I don't doubt it,' Latigo said. 'But that ain't why I mentioned Macahan.'

'Go on.'

'I will. But first, what about Drifter?'

Gabe shrugged. 'I could maybe persuade him to help. Like you said, he's got no love for Stadtlander either. That's if I can get hold of him.'

'That's why I mentioned Macahan,' Latigo said. 'I figure he could probably do that for us — 'long as we didn't say why we wanted Drifter.'

Gabe started to respond then paused as something struck him. He gave Latigo a suspicious, probing look. 'Wait a cotton minute,' he said. 'Now I get it.'

'Get what?' Waco asked.

'Why you skunks were so anxious to sober me up.'

'What're you talking about?'

'You needed me sober in order to get Clint Longley involved.'

'That's hogwash,' began Latigo.

'Save your breath,' Gabe snapped. 'It's so typical of you, I should've guessed right away.' Turning to Waco, he said: 'Mister, just tell me one thing: is your sob story about your brother true? Or is it all hot air that you and Lat made up so I'd help you with something bigger? Like a bank robbery or a Wells Fargo hold-up?'

'I swear it's the God's honest truth,' Waco replied.

'How do I know that?' Gabe demanded. 'You two jackals lied to me once, what's to stop you from lying again? I mean, where's your goddamn proof?'

Waco hesitated.

'Well?' Latigo demanded. 'What the hell you waiting for?'

Pinned, Waco slowly unbuttoned his shirt collar and bared the rope burn around his neck. 'This proof enough for you?' he asked quietly.

'Jesus.' Gabe winced, looked away and nodded. 'Okay,' he said. 'You've convinced me. Let's ride back to the U.S. and I'll wire Macahan to tell Drifter to meet us in Santa Rosa. I won't say why, I'll just tell the telegraph operator in El Paso to run it right over to the marshal's office. Clint will get it faster that way.'

'Thanks,' Waco said. 'I truly appreciate it.'

'Let's hope you still feel the same way when the lead starts flying,' Gabe said. 'Or when Stadlander tells the sheriff to round up a posse and stretch our necks.'

Waco shrugged, unperturbed. 'How many times can a fella hang?' he said grimly.

12

Early the next the day the three of them stood beside the railroad tracks near the abandoned, once-thriving mining town known as La Reina de Plata, some two miles east of Santa Rosa, waiting for the morning train from El Paso to arrive. Nearby, their saddled horses — along with an extra mount for Drifter — were tied to a dead tree, the gnarly roots of which poked from the bank of a dry creek bed.

The parched cracked earth wasn't much to look at now. But once, back in the early 1870s, tens of thousands of dollars' worth of gold dust and nuggets had been taken from the same creek by men willing to face scorching temperatures and vengeful Apaches.

But the gold soon ran out and the disenchanted prospectors began moving away — until one old-timer, who had stubbornly continued to pan for gold, discovered that the heavy gray-brown sand in the creek was primarily lead carbonate or cerussite, a rich silver-bearing ore. Despite his efforts to keep his strike a secret, word soon leaked out. It quickly spread throughout the territory, attracting swarms of miners. These men weren't content to just dig in the stream; they attacked the surrounding hills, sinking mine shafts that eventually led them to the mother lode. Suddenly a silver boom was on and the town, Silver Queen, was born.

But eventually the silver ran out, just like the gold, and this time everyone moved away, leaving the buildings to rot and the scarred hillsides overlooking the creek as the only reminder of man's greedy efforts to strike it rich.

'Here she comes now!' Latigo exclaimed as black smoke spiraled up behind the hills to the east.

'I hope to hell Drifter's on it,' Waco said to Gabe.

'Said he would be. That's good enough for me.'

'Why wouldn't he?' Latigo said. 'He knows we'd do the same for him.'

'Yeah, but you're his pals. Like I said before, he doesn't even know me.'

'I got a double eagle says he's aboard that train,' Gabe said. 'Any takers?'

'Not me,' Waco said.

Latigo scowled at Gabe. 'Where the hell did you get twenty dollars from? When I left you in Palomas just a short spell back you said you were dead broke.'

'I was,' Gabe replied. 'And still am.'

'Then how'd you get that gold — ?'

Gabe cut him off. 'That was drinking money I was talking about. This gold piece, it's strictly for emergencies.'

Latigo looked indignant. 'You call betting that Drifter's on that train an emergency?'

'Sure.'

'This lulu I got to hear.'

'It's simple,' Gabe said. 'If it comes down to a shootout 'tween us and

Stadlander's men, wouldn't you say it was an emergency to have an extra man along?'

'I reckon . . . '

'Well, Drifter's that extra man . . . which makes him an emergency.'

Latigo shook his head, exasperated. 'If you ain't got the damnedest, most twisted way of looking at things I ever come across then I'll eat my nose.' Pissed, he turned his back on Gabe and sulked.

Gabe winked at Waco, said: 'I'll go wait by the horses. If there's a lawman on that train I don't want him to see nothing but my backside.'

Twenty minutes later the train pulled up alongside Waco and Latigo. Steam hissed out from between the wheels into their faces, burning their eyes and forcing them to stumble back.

'Hurry it up, goddammit!' the engineer shouted testily at Waco and Latigo. 'I ain't got all day. Got a schedule to keep.'

'We ain't boarding,' Waco replied.

'We're waiting for a — '

'There he is now!' Latigo thumbed at a man who'd just alighted from the first passenger car. As tall as Gabe, he was whip-lean and darkly tanned from years in the saddle. No more than forty, if that, he had hawkish features and fierce gray eyes that radiated independence. Hatless, he wore a faded khaki shirt and Union cavalry pants tucked into Apache knee-high moccasins and carried his saddle as if it were weightless.

'C'mon,' Latigo said. 'Sooner we make dust, safer it'll be for Gabe.' He led the way toward Drifter, Waco following.

Seeing them leave the engineer released the brake and eased the throttle forward, the giant steel wheels spinning as they tried to get traction. It took a few moments but gradually the weight of the massive engine enabled the wheels to grip the rails and the locomotive, grunting like an old man straining, slowly pulled away.

13

Once introductions were over, the four of them rode in the direction of Santa Rosa. They rode at an easy, mile-consuming lope, Latigo and Drifter in the lead, Waco and Gabe following. No one spoke.

Waco used the silence to size up Drifter. Other than his impressive height, there was really nothing unusual about him — except for a certain aura that Waco found intriguing. He sensed it spoke of a calm, unyielding discipline and integrity that neither bribery nor torture could dissuade Drifter from completing whatever task he'd set himself.

Waco found the man's quiet strength and self-confidence comforting and though there were only four of them, for the first time he did not feel concerned by the thought of confronting Stadtlander or Jason Prince about the lynching of his brother.

When they neared Santa Rosa, they did not enter town but rode around the outskirts so as not to be seen by Sheriff Forbes or his deputy, knowing that if they were spotted by either lawman chances were that Stadtlander would be tipped off that they were coming.

Once they reached the hot open scrubland it was a thirty-minute ride to the big arched gateway that told everyone they were now entering land owned by the Double S. Nailed to the gateway was a sign that warned all trespassers would be shot on sight.

On reaching the gateway, they dismounted to give the horses a blow while they tried to figure out the best way to capture Jason without causing an all-out shootout.

Latigo, who believed killing was the best way to settle any argument, was pessimistic from the start. 'Save your breath,' he said before they could come up with a plan. 'There ain't no way to do this without lead flying. Hell, even if we managed to jump Jason when he was alone and threatened to shoot him if anyone else interferes, Stadtlander would still never let us go peacefully.'

'You sure about that?' Waco asked.

'Damn right,' Latigo replied. 'I know the man. He'd have to call our bluff whether he wanted to or not. His ego would insist on it. He'd be too afraid that if he didn't, not only his men but everyone in Santa Rosa would claim he'd gone soft . . . and from then on he'd never be able to intimidate anyone who tried to stand up to him. You follow?'

'Lat's right,' agreed Gabe. 'Stadtlander's whole life revolves around being able to bully folks into doing what he wants them to do.'

'So where does that leave us?'

For a moment no one had the answer. Then:

'What if we grabbed Slade as well as Jason?' said Drifter. 'You figure Stadtlander would be willing to sacrifice his foreman for the life of his only son?'

Gabe shrugged. 'It's possible. Since his daughter died, Slade's meant everything to him — even though he knows what a spoiled, lousy excuse for a son he is. On the other hand,' he added after a pause, 'I suppose it's also possible that due to all the trouble Slade has caused — the repeated drunken brawls and rapes he's accused of, not to mention all the times he and the Iverson brothers have shot up Santa Rosa just for the hell of it — Stadtlander might just be glad to be rid of the miserable sonofabitch.'

'What do you think?' Drifter asked Latigo. 'You know him better than us.'

The little Texas gunman shrugged. 'It's hard to say. Knowing how unpredictable the old man is, I wouldn't want to bet the farm on it either way. Could easily depend on the mood he happened to be in or how many times recently he's had to bail Slade out. But if my soul depended on it, I'd say Slade's life was still worth more than Prince's.'

'In that case,' Gabe said, 'I say, let's grab 'em both and take our chances. I mean, hell, it ain't like we got a lot of options.'

'We could always shoot him,' Latigo said.

'Slade, y'mean?'

'No, the old man. Cut off the head and the snake dies, as they say.'

'Yeah, but if we do that,' Drifter said, 'we'd not only have to fight off his men in order to make it out of there, but whoever pulled the trigger would then spend the rest of his life dodging the law as a murderer.'

'So let Gabe do it,' Latigo said. He turned to Gabriel Moonlight, adding: 'You're already facing a rope. What difference does it make whether it's for being a horse thief or a murderer?'

'Plenty,' Gabe replied. 'Murdering an unarmed man and shooting him in a gunfight are two mighty different things. And I ain't crossing that line for no one.'

'And we'd never ask you to,' Drifter

said. 'So — ' He stopped as Waco cursed aloud.

'What's wrong?' Gabe asked him.

'I just remembered something,' Waco said. 'I was supposed to ride out to the Double S with the sheriff this morning.'

'You what?' exclaimed Latigo.

Waco quickly repeated the conversation he'd had with Sheriff Forbes yesterday and the lawman's suggestion that Waco ride out with him to the Double S.

'Jesus,' Gabe said. 'Sure would've been nice to know that 'fore we got started.'

'I'm sorry,' Waco said. 'With everything else going on, it slipped my mind.'

'That puts a whole different slant on things,' Drifter said.

'Damn right it does,' agreed Gabe. 'Means we'll have to buck Lonnie Forbes as well as Stadtlander and his men.'

'I don't fancy having to gun down a lawman,' said Latigo. 'Not even a miserable sack of puss like Forbes. The consequences could be fatal.'

'We may not have a choice,' Drifter said. 'Stands to reason the sheriff ain't going to stand idly by while we drag Jason Prince away.' He checked his time piece before adding to Waco: 'You say you were supposed to meet Forbes at eight o'clock?'

Waco nodded.

'It's quarter after ten now. Which means it'll be around eleven-thirty by the time we reach the ranch-house.'

'What're you getting at?' Gabe asked him.

Drifter shrugged. 'Could be by that time the sheriff will have already finished his business with Stadtlander and is either riding back to town or on his way elsewhere.'

'My luck ain't that good,' Latigo said grimly. 'More likely he and the old man will be enjoying their coffee and brandy on the front porch as we ride up.'

'Don't expect them to ask us to join 'em, either,' said Gabe.

'Listen,' Waco broke in. 'I got a better

idea. I got you fellas into this, so it's only right I'm the one who squares things.'

'Go on,' Drifter said.

'Well, I was thinking . . . if Sheriff Forbes didn't recognize me after the lynching, chances are neither will Prince.'

'So?'

'Maybe if I was to ride in by my lonesome and pretend to be looking for work, like I told the sheriff, I might get a chance to talk to Prince alone. And if I do, I could stick a blade 'tween his ribs and be out of there before anyone figures out what's happened.'

There was silence as the other three men mulled over his suggestion. Then:

'Might work,' Latigo admitted. ''Specially if the sheriff puts in a good word for you, like he said he might.'

'You'd have to kill Prince somewhere you could quickly cover up his body,' Drifter said. 'You know, like in the barn or some other place that ain't out in the open.'

'Supposing there's no work and you can't talk to him alone?' Gabe said. 'What then?'

'I'll just ride out of there, smooth as you please.'

'What about us?' Drifter said. 'What're we supposed to be doing all this time?'

'Yeah,' Latigo chimed in. 'What are we going to be doing?'

'Nothing,' Waco said. 'Soon as I leave, you three ride back to town and I'll try to hook up with you later. Truth is,' he added when no one spoke, 'I've said all along that this is my problem and I should be the one to handle it. Or die trying. You can see that, can't you?'

The other swapped glances. His words made sense. There was no denying that.

'Tell you what,' Gabe said. 'I don't know what these other *hombres* figure on doing, but I'll be holed up at Ingrid Bjorkman's place. If you get out of this with your hide still intact, stop by. There'll be a pot of coffee brewing.'

'Much obliged,' Waco said. Then to Drifter: 'I don't know what to say, 'cept I'm right sorry for having you make a long train ride for nothing. Maybe one day I'll find a way to pay you back.'

'Forget it,' Drifter said. 'I was planning on coming up this way soon anyways. There's an auction starting in a few days at the Osage Horse Farm in Deming, and my daughter figured I might pick up a broodmare or two to breed with our Morgan stud.'

'Hell, if you're going to Deming,' Latigo said, 'then count me in. I got no use for a broodmare but there's a pretty little filly that lives there who might enjoy having her bed warmed by a handsome fella like me.'

'Filly, hell,' said Drifter. 'She must be an old, blind, toothless mare if she wants any part of you.'

Latigo waited for Gabe and Waco to stop laughing before replying. 'If you believe that, Ace, then I reckon you don't want me to set you up with her twin sister?'

'Oh, I dunno,' Drifter drawled as Gabe and Waco laughed even harder. 'You could probably twist my arm and I 'spect I'd be willing take her off your hands.'

'Don't do me any favors,' Latigo grumbled. He turned to Waco, adding: 'You sure you want to go ahead with this, *amigo*? I mean, there'll be plenty of other times to brace Stadtlander or Prince when the law ain't present.'

'Thanks,' Waco said. 'But I've come too far to turn back now.' To Gabe and Drifter he added: 'Again, thanks for offering to back my play.'

'Anytime,' said Drifter.

'Just remember,' Gabe warned Waco. 'Killing a lawman — any lawman — always leads to a necktie party.'

'I'll be sure to keep that in mind,' Waco said. He gave a throwaway salute, mounted his sorrel and rode on through the gateway . . . onto Double S property.

14

Stadtlander's impressive, Western-style ranch-house stood on a flat-topped grassy knoll that was completely fenced in. The wealthy rancher had built the fancy, three-story mansion there for two reasons: in the early days, it was so he could see any Apaches or Comancheros approaching; and years later, when the Indians had been subdued and his hired gunmen had forced out all the surrounding ranchers, he wanted the rest of the territory to see how rich and important he'd become.

As Waco rode past the outer corrals and on between the barn and two bunkhouses, where a bunch of hands were busy with chores, he saw that Latigo's grim premonition had been right: for there on the wide first-floor veranda that ran all the way around the big square house sat Sheriff Forbes, drinking coffee laced with brandy with a short, stocky man in his early seventies that Waco guessed was Stillman J. Stadtlander.

Several of the hands buckled on their gun-belts when they saw Waco ride in. Not wanting to give them any excuse to shoot him, he kept his hand away from his six-gun and tried to ignore them as they closed in behind him.

Ahead, Waco saw Stadtlander set his cup down and pick up the rifle leaned against the railing. Levering in a round, the rancher laid the Winchester across his lap and studied Waco as he slowly drew closer.

Waco returned the favor, focusing solely on Stadtlander as he rode his horse at a slow walk up to the wealthy, ruthless rancher. Though not a big man, he commanded attention. He had thick wavy white hair and a square, jut-jawed, pugnacious face that resembled a pit bull. His body, once powerful, was now stoop-shouldered and plagued by gout. But despite his crippling ailment, he still looked capable of taking on anyone in any situation.

Waco saw Sheriff Forbes lean forward and say something to Stadtlander, who at once waved his men off and traded his belligerent, distrusting expression for one of curious interest.

'Step down, young fella,' he said as Waco reined up in front of him. Then as Waco obeyed and stood there, holding the reins, the thumb of his right hand tucked into his belt: 'Sheriff, here, says you're looking for work?'

'Yes, sir.'

'Where'd you last draw wages?'

'The Running Bar-Z.'

'I know Reed Ketchum. Good man. Why'd he fire you?'

'He didn't, sir. I quit.'

'How come? Ketchum's a fair and reasonable fella to work for.'

'I know, sir. Personal reasons.'

Stadtlander nodded as if accepting the answer. Continuing to size up Waco, he said: 'Sheriff Forbes says he told you

I didn't need any hands.'

'Yes, sir.'

'Yet you rode all the way out here anyways? Why?'

Waco smiled, not fooled by the rancher's seemingly innocuous question.

'I'm sure you already know why, Mr. Stadtlander. But in case the sheriff neglected to mention it, I was hoping one of your men had quit unexpectedly and you needed to replace him.'

'Then you're fresh out of luck, son, 'cause nobody's quit that I know of.'

Rather than backing off, Waco said: 'You should hire me anyway, Mr. Stadtlander.'

'Oh?' The rancher looked amused by Waco's directness. 'Why's that?'

'Because I'm a top hand, sir. I'm loyal, I'm a hard worker and I never complain. Just ask Reed Ketchum. He'll tell you. He believed in me. If he hadn't, he wouldn't have made me foreman over several more experienced men.'

'Foreman, huh?'

'Yes, sir.'

Impressed, Stadtlander pointed at the barn, said: 'Go talk to Jason Prince. Tell him if he can find work for you, I won't object.'

'Yes, sir.' Waco tipped his hat. 'Thanks, Mr. Stadtlander. You won't regret it.'

'If I do,' the rancher warned, 'you'll regret it even more.' He turned back to the table, signifying that he was done talking, and Waco led his horse toward the barn.

* * *

Jason Prince wasn't in the barn. But the rear doors were open and through them Waco saw the burly foreman, shirtless and bent over a trough, washing his upper body.

Blood pounding in his ears, Waco unhooked the safety strap on his holstered gun and prepared to draw should Prince recognize him.

But as the foreman straightened up and saw Waco, he didn't react. He only thumbed at a towel draped over the pump and in a gravelly voice said: 'Hand me that, mister.'

Waco obeyed. He'd had many fights in his life, once even knifing a drunken hand who'd attacked him, but he'd never killed anyone before and the thought of gunning down Prince, even though the man had helped lynch his brother, Chris, unnerved him — even sickened him some.

'Who are you, mister, and what do you want?' Prince asked as he dried off.

'Name's Waco McCullum. I just spoke to Mr. Stadtlander. He told me to tell you that if you could use another hand, he wouldn't object to you hiring me.'

Prince frowned, surprised. 'Be damned to hell'n back. He said that, did he?'

'He did.'

'You know the boss from someplace else, do you?'

'Uh-uh.'

'How 'bout your folks? Did they once do him a favor, making him beholden to you?'

'Nope.'

'See, the reason I ask is, just two days ago I let a good man go 'cause we had no work for him. Odd, wouldn't you say?'

Waco shrugged. 'I'm just telling you what Mr. Stadtlander said.'

'Oh, I don't doubt that. Hell, there wouldn't be much point in you lying, mister, not when all I got to do is ask the boss myself.'

Waco saw no reason to reply. He just stood there, looking at Prince while at the same time trying to see if they were alone behind the barn or if there were other men nearby who might see him stab the foreman or pistol-whip him to death.

He couldn't see anyone. But before he could decide on the best way to kill Prince, he heard voices approaching. He froze as two hands came hurrying around the barn. On seeing their foreman, they blurted out that one of the men, Walt Raimy, had just been thrown from his horse and was 'busted up pretty bad, boss.'

Jason Prince turned to Waco and shook his head as if he couldn't believe the news. 'Seems like your lucky day all around, friend.' Then to one of the men: 'Show this new man where to stow his gear in the bunkhouse, Roy.'

'Sure thing, boss.'

Waco said to Prince: 'If it's okay with you, I need to ride back into town to get my things. But I'll be back 'fore nightfall.'

'Be sure you are,' Prince said. He and the other two men then hurried off around the barn, leaving Waco standing there, wondering if this really was his lucky day . . . or if Fate had merely delayed what he inevitably had to do.

15

Stadtlander and Sheriff Forbes were no longer drinking coffee on the veranda by the time Waco rode past the mansion. Instead, a white-coated Mexican servant was gathering up the cups, saucers and brandy bottle and putting them on a tray beside an elegant silver coffee pot. Also, the sheriff's horse was gone from the nearby tie-rail and Waco guessed the lawman had headed back to town.

Waco nudged the sorrel toward the front gate. Several hands repairing a corral fence paused to study Waco as he rode past, their expressions full of curiosity. He guessed they were wondering, like Jason Prince, why Stadtlander had agreed to hire a stranger after cutting loose an experienced hand.

Waco couldn't help wondering the

same thing. Admittedly the sheriff had probably put in a good word for him, but from what Latigo had told him about the lawman's relationship with Stadtlander, Waco didn't think the rancher was unduly influenced by Forbes' opinion. And if that was true, what was the real reason for Stadlander's decision?

Before Waco could think of any logical reason, he saw three riders approaching the gate. He recognized them immediately but had to take a second look just to be sure he wasn't imagining things.

Reining in, he waited for them to ride up to him before asking: 'What the hell are you doing here?'

'Making sure you got out of here in one piece,' Latigo said.

'But I thought — '

'Exactly what we wanted you to think,' finished Gabe.

'What he means is,' Drifter added as Waco looked confused, 'we wanted you to play your hand as you saw fit, and not because of us being there with you.'

'Clint's right,' Latigo said. 'Sometimes a fella has to ride lonesome in order to truly figure out what's on his mind. Then once everything's clear to him, he can either leave his iron holstered or go ahead and pull the trigger knowing he can't live with himself if he don't. You follow?'

'In other words,' Waco said, 'you figured I might not have the sand to kill Prince if I was by myself, but would if you three were there backing me up?'

'No, that ain't it at all,' Gabe corrected. 'No one's questioning your grit. You're man enough to cast your own shadow without our help. No, this is all about giving you time to straighten out your brains, so you can think clearly and don't regret shooting a fella after it's too late to change your mind.'

'And since I don't hear any kind of ruckus,' Drifter chimed in, 'I'd say you already made that choice.'

'I didn't get the chance,' Waco said. 'The choice was made for me.' He briefly explained what happened and why he hadn't killed Jason Prince. 'But now that I'm going to be working here steady,' he concluded, 'I don't have to rush things but can take my own sweet time about avenging my brother.'

'Now I call that smart thinking,' Latigo said.

Gabe and Drifter nodded in agreement.

'It'll also give you time to find out exactly whose beef it was your brother and his pal supposedly rustled,' Latigo reminded.

'And if he was telling you the truth about this other fella being involved,' Gabe said.

'Chris would never lie to me,' Waco said firmly. 'I taught him better than that.'

'I'm sure you did,' Drifter said. 'All Lat's saying is, you want the God's own truth in your heart when it comes time to put a bullet in Jason Prince!'

Seeing the wisdom in that, Waco nodded and then explained that he had to return to Santa Rosa to pick up his gear.

'We'll ride along with you,' Latigo said. 'Maybe buy you a farewell drink before going our separate ways.'

'Not me,' Gabe said. 'I'll be leaving you at the Bjorkman spread. It's already been too long since I spent time with Ingrid.'

Drifter chuckled and winked at Latigo and Waco. 'Amazing how the thought of a pretty woman can corrupt a perfectly good man, ain't it?'

Gabe waited for them to stop laughing before saying: 'If that's your idea of corruption, *compadre*, it's no wonder you're still driftin'.'

'You got me there,' Drifter admitted. 'Truth is, *amigo*, I'm just jealous — '

His words were cut off by a rifle shot.

Instantly, Waco's sorrel lurched and stumbled, took another step and went down. It happened so suddenly Waco was thrown from the saddle.

Gabe, Latigo and Drifter quickly reined up and dismounted, grabbed their rifles and pulled their horses down to the ground. Taking cover behind them, the four men scanned the mostly-flat horizon in an effort to see who'd fired the shot.

'I don't see nobody,' Waco said. 'Do you?'

Gabe, Drifter and Latigo shook their heads.

'Probably hiding in one of those ravines or dry gulches,' Latigo said.

'Or behind those rocks,' Gabe said, pointing at a distant rocky outcrop.

'Be one helluva shot from either place,' remarked Drifter. 'Must be almost a mile.'

'Has to be a Sharps,' said Latigo.

'And a heavy grain bullet,' Drifter added. ' — a 50–90 maybe.'

Waco, lying behind the body of his horse, looked at the blood pumping out from the big hole in the sorrel's neck and said: 'You'll get no argument from me.'

'Which means he can shoot us but we can't shoot him,' Gabe said grimly.

'Doesn't make sense,' Drifter said. Then as the others looked at him: 'Fella who can make a shot like that doesn't miss what he's aiming at.'

'You saying he wasn't trying to kill me?' Waco said.

'That'd be my guess.'

'Then what the hell's his point? I mean why kill a horse for no reason?'

'Maybe it's a warning,' Gabe suggested.

'For me not to do what?' Waco asked.

'Sign on with the Double S.'

'That means the shooter's got to be Jason Prince,' Waco said, ''cause I don't know anybody else working there.'

'You sure Stadtlander didn't recognize you?' Drifter said.

Waco nodded. 'I'd stake my life on it.'

'From the way you explained it,' said Gabe, 'Prince didn't recognize you either.'

'If he did, he sure didn't show it,'

Waco agreed. 'But if the shooter ain't Prince or one of the Double S boys, who the hell is it? And why didn't he kill me instead of my horse? And if it *is* a warning, like you say,' he said to Latigo, 'it's a pretty vague one. I mean what if I didn't catch on? What's his next step — shooting me when no one's around, then burying me and telling everyone in Santa Rosa that I quit and rode off?'

'Reckon that's as good a guess as any,' Drifter said.

No one spoke for a few moments. The only sound was the soft moan of the wind as it blew tiny swirls of sand past them.

'Well,' Latigo said finally, 'I don't have the answer, but I sure got the solution: brace the bear in his cave.'

'Confront Stadtlander, you mean?' Gabe asked.

'Him — *and* Jason Prince. Threaten to shoot the bastards unless they come clean.'

'Jesus,' Gabe said. 'You're just itching

to pull the trigger on someone, ain't you?'

Latigo shrugged. 'If you got a better idea, *amigo*, let's hear it — now — 'fore that fella with the Sharps decides not to miss the next one of us he aims at.'

'For once I agree with him,' said Drifter. 'We're sitting ducks out here.'

'Whoa,' Waco said, 'it's me he's warning, not you three.'

'Let's hope you're right,' Gabe said.

'So how do you want to play this?' Latigo asked him.

'I'm going to give him another shot at me,' Waco said. 'I'm going to start walking toward town. If he doesn't shoot, then my guess is he won't fire at any of you either. He'll figure I understood the warning and let it go at that. Then, after I've gone a ways, you catch up with me and I'll ride on into town with you.'

'And then?' Latigo demanded.

'I'm going to buy another horse, wait until dark and then ride back to the ranch.'

'And do what?' inquired Gabe.

'Find a way to get Prince and Stadtlander together and force the truth out of them.'

'I'll go with you,' Latigo said. 'Jason and the old man know me well enough not to pull a fast one.'

'We'll all go,' Drifter chimed in. 'Get this mess straightened out once and for all.'

'I appreciate the offer,' Waco said, 'but you truly don't have to. None of you.'

'We're going,' Latigo said firmly. 'End of sermon.'

16

When the four of them rode through the gate and reined up in front of Stadtlander's house, neither Prince nor any of the hands tried to stop them. Waco wasn't surprised. The men he was riding with had widespread reputations as shootists and though Latigo was the only one who enjoyed killing, none of the Double S hands was anxious to test the other two.

But one man did run into the house. Moments later Stadtlander and Prince emerged and stood side-by-side on the veranda. Both were armed with scatter-guns and kept them aimed at Waco and the others as Stadtlander demanded to know what they wanted.

'You got the nerve to ask me that,' Waco growled, 'after shooting my goddamn horse out from under me?'

Stadtlander and Prince swapped

puzzled looks, then the rancher turned back to Waco, saying: 'You got your ropes knotted, son. We had nothing to do with killing your horse.'

'Nor did anyone who works here,' Prince said. 'I'll vouch for every one of them. So why don't you just turn around and ride out of here 'fore I blast you out of that saddle!'

Latigo whitened and his left hand hovered above one of his ivory-handled Colts. 'You'll be dead long before that,' he warned softly. 'And so will your boss.'

'Easy,' Drifter said. 'Everybody take a deep breath. This don't have to be settled with lead.'

'But it does have to be settled,' added Gabe.

'And how do you plan on doing that?' Prince asked.

'That's easy,' Waco said. 'You and your boss can start by telling me which of your men owns a Sharps rifle.'

'No one that I know of,' replied Stadtlander. 'D'you, Jason?'

'No, sir.' Prince turned to Waco. 'My men are wranglers and cattle punchers, not buffalo hunters.'

'How 'bout bushwhackers?' Latigo prodded. 'Or is that just limited to you?'

Prince went white but somehow controlled himself. 'I ain't drawing against you, Rawlins, no matter what you call me.'

'How 'bout me?' Waco said. 'Or are you too yellow to face anyone who can shoot back?'

'Jason,' Stadtlander said as his enraged foreman looked as if he might draw, 'I'm ordering you to get back to work! Now, goddammit,' he growled when Prince didn't respond. 'I pay you to run this ranch, not settle gunfights!'

'But Mr. Stadtlander — '

'You heard me, mister. Get off this porch and earn your damn wages!'

Bottling his rage, Prince stepped off the veranda and started toward the barn.

Waco let him take a few steps and

then rammed him with his horse, sending the foreman sprawling.

It was too humiliating for Prince to ignore. Not bothering to pick up the dropped shotgun, he scrambled up, grabbed Waco's leg and jerked him from the saddle.

Waco hit the dirt, rolled over and got halfway to his knees when Prince dived at him. Both men went flying. They were up almost as quickly and began swinging wildly. They were too angry for their punches to do any damage and, frustrated, they finally lunged at each other and wrestled one another to the ground. There, they grappled, rolling over and over, each trying to get a choke-hold.

Some of the hands now came running up. But Drifter, Gabe and Latigo trained their weapons on them, keeping them back.

The fight continued, but neither Waco nor Prince was able to get the upper hand.

Suddenly a shot rang out.

Everyone turned toward the front gate as Sheriff Forbes, smoking pistol in hand, came riding up.

'Call your man off,' he told Latigo, Gabe and Drifter. 'Or I'll be forced to stop him myself.' He wagged his six-gun threateningly at them.

Smirking, Latigo said: 'Go ahead, you big tub of lard. I've been looking for a legitimate excuse to put a round into that soft belly of yours for years.'

The sheriff paled and quickly holstered his gun.

Stadtlander looked disgusted. 'You may be fast,' he told Latigo, 'but not even you can shoot all of us before one of us gets you. So why not be reasonable and break this up 'fore someone gets killed?'

'Do as he says, Lat,' Gabe said. 'Leather your iron. Bucking the law ain't going to get us what we want.' Dismounting, he grabbed Waco and dragged him off Prince.

Once on his feet, Waco jerked himself free and glared at Sheriff Forbes. 'This man,' he said, thumbing at Prince, 'shot my horse. What're you going to do about it?'

'That true?' the sheriff asked Prince.

''Course it ain't true,' the foreman said. His face was cut and bleeding from Waco's blows and his knuckles were skinned. ''Cording to him the animal was shot by a Sharps, and you won't find a long gun anywhere on this spread no matter how hard you look.'

'He's telling the truth, son,' the sheriff told Waco. 'I been coming out here for many a year and never once did I see anyone with a Sharps. Fact is,' he added, 'only man in the whole territory that owns one to my knowledge is Mr. McKinley — '

'Jory McKinley?' Stadtlander said, surprised.

'Yes, sir. Took it off the wall and showed it to me once when I talked to him 'bout some cattle he'd lost to rustlers. Said he used to be a buffalo hunter back in the late '60s.'

'Huh, I never knew that,' Stadtlander

said, adding: 'While we're on the subject of McKinley, Lonnie, tell Waco, here, about the evidence that Jory gave you.'

The sheriff turned back to Waco. 'Mr. McKinley found a neckerchief bearing your brother's initials stuck on the horn of one of his steers.'

'That's what led the posse to Chris in the first place,' Stadtlander added. 'Isn't that right, Jason?'

Prince nodded. 'Yes, sir. Mr. McKinley showed it to me himself. There was no doubt it belonged to young McAllum. Which is why we felt justified stretching his neck.'

Waco had trouble arguing with that logic. 'This neckerchief,' he said uneasily, 'where is it now?'

'Back at my office,' Sheriff Forbes said. 'Be happy to show it to you any time you feel like dropping by.'

Shaken, Waco said: 'Even if what you say is true, that still don't prove nothing. Hell, there's a million different reasons from the wind on down, why my brother's neckerchief could have gotten stuck on that steer's horns.'

'Maybe. But that ain't the only proof,' Prince said. 'Mr. McKinley saw Chris and his pal stealing his beef. Says he shot Chris' horse out from under him and was moving in to grab him, when your brother jumped up behind his pal and rode off in the dark.'

Drifter, silent up till now, said: 'This McKinley fella — he got a spread around here somewhere?'

'Yeah. Just a few miles from here. It shares boundaries with Mr. Stadtlander's southern range. That's why our beef was on his land. They often wander over there. Same with Mr. McKinley's cattle.'

'Happens so often,' Stadtlander explained, 'we don't even bother to send 'em back. We keep them until roundup time, then cut them out and make the swap.'

'So the beef my brother rustled actually belonged to you,' Waco said, 'not this Jory McKinley?'

'Damn right. That's why my men knew Chris was lying.'

'It's also why he and his pal were using a running iron,' put in Prince, ' — to change the brand that was already on our cattle.'

'Change it to what?'

'That we don't know.'

Waco thought a moment before saying: 'Why do you think Chris tried to involve that fella on the blue roan?'

'That's obvious,' Prince said. 'To shift the blame onto Mr. McKinley.'

'But he didn't shift blame. He just said McKinley was as guilty as he was.'

'That's another lie,' Stadtlander said. 'Jory's as honest as the day is long. I know. I've had business dealings with him for years.'

'Dealings which you've always come out on the short end,' reminded Prince.

Stadtlander shrugged. 'So he's smarter than me. No crime in that.'

Waco, as the thought hit him, said: 'So this Jory McKinley is definitely the fella riding that blue roan?'

'Yeah. Why?'

Waco smiled as if it was all starting to make sense. 'One last thing,' he said to Stadtlander. 'Can you or your foreman show me what McKinley's brand looks like?'

Stadtlander nodded to Prince, who knelt on one knee and with his forefinger drew the Lazy B brand in the dirt.

Waco studied it for a few moments. Then, satisfied by what he saw, he mounted his horse. 'Be seeing you, Mr. Stadtlander. C'mon,' he told Latigo, Gabe and Drifter. 'I got some riding to do.'

'Hold it!' barked Sheriff Forbes. He waited until the four riders reined up and faced him, then spoke directly to Gabe: 'I ain't forgetting you're a wanted man, Moonlight. Next time you cross the border, I'll have a rope waiting for you.'

'Why wait?' Gabe replied. 'Why not hang me now?'

The sheriff licked his lips uneasily.

'You're awful brave, mister, when you got Latigo Rawlins backing your play.'

'Lat,' Gabe told the dapper little bounty hunter, 'no matter how this turns out, I don't want you interfering. You got that?'

'Sure,' Latigo said. 'You don't need my help anyway. Not against this gutless weasel.'

Gabe turned back to the lawman. 'Satisfied, Lonnie?'

The sheriff swallowed, hard, but said nothing.

'What're you waiting for?' Gabe asked him. 'Get to the hanging.'

Stadtlander, realizing the sheriff had backed himself into a corner, said quickly: 'There'll be no gunplay here! Or hanging! As for you four,' he told Gabe and the others, 'get off my property. Now!'

Gabe laughed mockingly at the shamed lawman. 'You wriggled off the hook today, Lonnie. But next time we meet, trust me, you won't be so lucky.'

He swung his horse around and

joined Waco, Latigo and Drifter. 'Reckon we've out-stayed our welcome, gents. Let's ride.'

The four of them dug in their spurs and rode off.

Stadtlander watched them ride out through the gate and then turned to the sheriff.

'Next time you shoot off your mouth, don't expect me to save your sorry ass.'

'Mr. Stadtlander, I didn't ask — '

'Shut up, damn you!' Stadtlander wagged his finger at the lawman. 'You're nothing but a goddamn joke, Lonnie. You know it. I know it. All of Santa Rosa knows it. And a joke, especially an unfunny one, is something I can't afford!' He stormed off into the house.

17

After leaving Gabe at the Bjorkman spread, Waco, Latigo and Drifter rode on into Santa Rosa. There, at the little brown-and-yellow station-house, Drifter and Latigo bought tickets to Deming. The next train wasn't until late afternoon, so they joined Waco for a farewell drink at Rosario's. Afterward, Waco left Latigo and Drifter in the busy cantina and crossed the street to Georgina's rooming house.

Danny was seated behind the front desk, amusing herself with a box of crayons and a coloring book.

'Want to see what I done?' she said as Waco entered and leaned on the desk.

'Sure.'

She turned the book around so the pages faced him. Waco looked at the picture she'd been coloring. It showed a clutch of chickens in a barnyard. The hens and chicks were busy feeding while a rooster sat atop a fence, proudly crowing. Though the rooster and chickens were drawn realistically, their colors were as vivid and varied as a rainbow.

'My goodness,' Waco exclaimed. 'This here's beautiful.'

'You really think so? I mean, you ain't saying it just 'cause you like my mother?'

'Liking your ma has nothing to do with liking your crayoning, Danny. Even if I didn't like your ma, I'd still like the picture. Got my word on that.'

'What about the chickens?'

'What about them?'

'Do you like the colors I made them?'

'I sure do.'

'Better than what real chickens look like?'

'Much better. Regular chickens are kind of . . . uhm' — he searched for a word that wouldn't offend her — 'drab-looking. Yours ain't.'

'No,' Danny agreed, 'they surely ain't.' She admired her work for a moment before adding: ''Course, they aren't as real-looking either.'

'True.'

'But I bet if you asked them chickens what colors they'd like to be, they'd choose my colors too.'

'I know I would,' Waco said. 'But that really ain't the point. The point is you're the artist. You decide what colors you want the chickens to be. That's why they call it art.'

'Yeah?' Danny screwed up her face as she considered his remark. 'Then I reckon I'm a real artist, ain't I?'

''Aren't' I,' corrected her mother as she came from the parlor and joined her daughter at the desk.

Danny rolled her eyes at Waco. 'Don't mind Momma. She's from Boston where they all talk polite and proper. Not like us ignorant folks out here in the west.'

'That's quite enough out of you, young lady,' Georgie said. Then to

Waco: 'Good afternoon, Mr. McAllum. Nice to see you again.'

'See what I mean?' Danny said to Waco. 'So polite it makes you sick.' She ducked under the playful swipe her mother aimed at her and ran into the parlor.

Georgie shook her head at Waco. 'As you can see, Mr. McAllum, Daniella and I are somewhat at odds when it comes to English grammar.'

Waco chuckled. 'I'm glad you weren't around when I was growing up. I would've been black and blue all over.'

'I doubt that,' Georgie said. 'From what Daniella tells me, your mother was a schoolteacher.'

'She was indeed.'

'Then I can't believe you got away with even half as much as Daniella does.'

Waco chuckled again. 'Let's just say that sometimes a certain part of me felt tender when I sat down to supper.'

They both laughed.

'Would you care for a room?' Georgie then asked.

'No, I'm on my way somewheres.'

'Oh.' She frowned, disappointed. 'You came in just to see Daniella then?'

'Uh-uh. Truth is I came in to ask you something.'

'Me?' Georgie looked surprised and pleased. 'Well, then, by all means ask away.'

'It's personal, so if you don't feel like answering, I'll understand, ma'am.'

Georgie smiled. 'I'm sure it'll be all right. It would also be all right if you called me Georgie. I feel we're well enough acquainted by now to use first names.'

'That suits me fine,' Waco said.

'So what's your question?'

'I'd like you to describe what Judd McCutcheon looks like.'

It was the last thing Georgie was expecting. 'J-Judd? My ex-husband?'

'If you don't mind, ma'am — Georgie.'

'N-No, of course not, but — may I

ask why you want to know, Mr. McAllum?'

'Waco.'

'Waco.'

''Cause he might be using another name now. And if he is, I'd like to know 'cause I got dealings with him.'

'Dealings?'

'Yeah. It's too complicated to explain right now, but it would sure help me if I knew whether he and this other fella were one and the same.'

'I see . . . W-Well,' she stammered, 'I — he was, you know, fairly average-looking.'

'Tall, short, fat, lean . . . ?'

'Tall — about your height or maybe an inch shorter. Heavier than you, but by no means fat. Just a big-boned burly man.'

'Dark or fair?'

'Neither. His ancestors were Celtic, and from them he got his coloring. Of course I haven't seen Judd for . . . well, for some time now but I can't imagine that he's gone gray overnight. His hair was reddish, thick and very straight . . . and when he wasn't wearing a hat it used to hang down in front sometimes . . . you know, over his forehead like a fringe. His eyes were greenish-blue, though some people called them hazel, and no matter how often he shaved, he always had a slight beard — no, not a beard exactly, more like a . . . '

'Stubble?'

'Yes. That's it. His six o'clock shadow he used to call it.'

Waco nodded. 'Anything else about him I should know?'

'N-No, I don't think so — oh, wait a minute. There is something. Judd always dressed like an English — no, Scottish squire. He also had a habit of tugging on his ear, like this' — she tugged on the lobe of her left ear — 'just before he said or did something important. He wasn't aware of it, I don't think. It was just one of those, you know, subconscious habits he had . . . like gritting his teeth or clenching his fists just before losing his temper.'

'Thanks. That could be very helpful,' Waco said. Then: 'Did he carry a gun?'

'You mean in his hand?'

'No. On his hip . . . like this?' He tapped his holster.

'Uhm . . . no, I don't ever remember Judd carrying a gun that way. But he did possess a gun and he kept it with him at all times.'

'Where?'

'Under his coat — a shoulder holster, I think he called it.' She paused, uncomfortable discussing her ex-husband, then said: 'Just one more thing. If this other man *is* Judd, I advise you be very wary of him. He has the most dreadful temper and was always losing it over the slightest things. So I'd be most careful about not annoying him.'

'I'll keep that mind, ma'am.'

'Georgie.'

'Georgie.' Waco grinned again. 'Reckon we're having trouble remembering each other's first names.'

'Hopefully we'll soon get over that,' she said. Then as if embarrassed by voicing her thoughts, she quickly added: 'I hope I'm not being too forward, Waco?'

'Not a bit,' he said. 'Truth is — *Georgie* — by the time I get back I'll have no problem remembering you or your first name.' Tipping his hat, he turned and went to the door. Opening it, he looked back at her and grinned. 'Tell that daughter of yourn that from now on I'll never look at chickens the same way again.' He was gone, the tiny bell tinkling as the door closed behind him.

Georgie stared after him and gave a long resigned sigh.

'You like him, huh, Momma?'

Georgie turned and found Danny watching her from the parlor doorway.

'Y-Yes, I do,' Georgie said after a pause. 'Very much.'

'Much as you did pa?'

Her mother frowned sadly. 'No, dear. But then I doubt if I will ever feel quite the love I felt for your father again. That was a . . . once-in-a-lifetime experience.

However, that doesn't mean I couldn't like or love another man in a different way.' She turned back to the front door, as if hoping Waco would magically reappear. 'As for Mr. McAllum ... well, I'd be lying if I didn't admit that I hope he returns soon ... safe and sound.'

18

Sheriff Forbes sat behind his desk cleaning and assembling his pearl-handled Colt .45, with its custom 4-inch barrel that was known as a 'Sheriff's Special.' An oily cloth and a cleaning rod lay on the desk beside a half-empty mug of black coffee. He hummed quietly as he assembled the trigger guard, the noise similar to the buzzing of the two horse flies trapped against the window.

The sound of boots approaching along the boardwalk, followed by silence as they stopped outside his door, alerted the lawman that someone was about to enter.

He quickly reached into the open desk drawer and pulled out an old, long-barreled, single-action Peacemaker with deer-horn grips. Resting the gun on his lap, finger still on the trigger, he picked up the mug with the other hand and casually took a sip ... his eyes never leaving the door.

'You?' he said, surprised, as the door opened and Waco entered. 'I figured you'd be halfway to Texas by now.'

'You hoped, you mean?' Waco kept his hand away from his holstered six-gun as he approached the desk and saw the Peacemaker on the lawman's lap. 'What's the matter, sheriff, you expecting unfriendly company?'

'I didn't survive this long by falling asleep at the reins,' the lawman replied. He put the Peacemaker back in the drawer and finished assembling the trigger guard, adding: 'I'm sure you didn't come by to shoot the breeze, so why don't you get to the meat?'

'I want you to ride with me to McKinley's spread.'

'Why for do you want me to do that?'

''Cause I believe he's the brains behind both the rustling of Stadtlander's beef and altering his brand with a running iron.'

164

'Seems to me, mister, your brother was already hanged for both them things.'

'Doesn't mean he wasn't in cahoots with McKinley.'

'Go on.'

'Well, I hate to say this about my own brother, sheriff. But truthfully Chris wasn't smart enough to come up with a plan this clever all by his lonesome.'

Sheriff Forbes gave Waco a long, shrewd look. 'You just blowing more smoke or can you prove any of this?'

'I'm pretty sure I can prove it.'

The sheriff fastened the last screw, tested the firmness of the trigger guard and then gently, almost lovingly set the Colt on the desk before looking up at Waco.

'Want to tell me how?'

Waco answered by picking up a notepad and a pencil from the desk and quickly sketching something. The lawman, curious now, looked on in silence.

Waco showed the lawman the sketch.

'These are Stadtlander's and McKinley's brands, correct?'

'Close enough.'

Waco then altered Stadtlander's Double S brand by adding a loop to each tip of the S, and held up the finished drawing. It was identical now to McKinley's Lazy B brand.

''Be damned,' Sheriff Forbes said. 'Here, let me try that.' He took the pencil and paper from Waco and made a sketch of both brands. He then altered Stadtlander's brand by adding the two loops. 'Sonofabitch,' he breathed. 'Wonder why no one's ever figured that out before?'

'Someone did,' Waco said. 'Jory McKinley.'

The lawman grunted as if still not convinced by what he'd seen.

'What's more,' Waco continued, 'like I just said, I'm guessing McKinley and my brother were in this together.'

'I'm listening.'

'Well, the way I figure it, Chris and his pal rustled the beef and drove them onto McKinley's land. There they altered the brands and then turned the cattle loose among McKinley's herd.'

The sheriff mulled over Waco explanation, unconsciously twirling the ends of his mustache. 'Say you're right,' he said after a pause, 'what did your brother get out of it?'

Waco shrugged. 'He never said, but money would be my guess. Lots of it.'

'From McKinley?'

'Sure. He most likely paid Chris for each brand he changed.'

The lawman considered the idea for a few moments. Waco again heard the two horse flies buzzing as they repeatedly hurled themselves against the glass.

'Okay,' the sheriff said grudgingly. 'Say you're right on all counts. Who tipped us off so that we could catch 'em red-handed?'

'McKinley, who else?'

'But — '

'Let me finish. And again, this is only a guess. Knowing my brother and his

167

lust for money, he more than likely got greedy and demanded a bigger share of the profits.'

'He'd need leverage for that, wouldn't he? 'Sides, if he threatened to tell Mr. Stadtlander 'bout what was going on, he'd know he'd be putting his own head in the noose as well.'

'Not if he tipped Stadtlander off the way McKinley tipped you and the other lawmen off — by sending an unsigned note. Then it would be his word against McKinley's. And if I'm right about McKinley, which I think I am, he'd go to prison for a much longer spell than Chris, even if a judge decided that my brother was somehow involved.'

'Why?'

Waco hesitated.

Sheriff Forbes frowned suspiciously at him. 'What do you know about Mr. McKinley that you ain't telling me?'

'Ride with me and I'll explain everything along the way. I need you there,' Waco added as the lawman started to protest, 'so you can witness how McKinley reacts when I give him the good news.'

The sheriff nodded, as if picturing how McKinley would respond.

'Yeah,' he said, more to himself than to Waco. 'That ain't going to sit too kindly with him, that's for damn' sure.'

19

Dusk was closing in when they reached McKinley's ranch. The workday over, some of the weary hands were washing up, while others trooped into the bunkhouse, bellies aching for supper. None of them paid attention to Waco or Sheriff Forbes as they dismounted outside the two-story ranch-house. Though not as impressive as Stadtlander's mansion, the adobe-walled building with its Spanish-tiled roof and cathedral-shaped windows was still grand enough to put the neighboring log cabin ranch-houses to shame.

Jory McKinley emerged from the front door and stood there smiling as the sheriff and Waco joined him on the tiled porch. Dressed in tweed Scottish-style riding clothes, he looked pretty much as Georgina had described her former husband, except that the lower half of his face was now covered with a full auburn beard that hid most of his thin sneering mouth. But not even the beard could disguise the fact that this man was Judd McCutcheon, and Waco felt rage building inside him.

'I thought that was you, laddie,' McKinley said, shaking the sheriff's hand. 'Tell me now. What pleasurable occasion brings you to my neck of the woods?'

'I'm afraid it ain't for pleasure,' the lawman said. 'Waco, here, has brought some very serious charges against you, Mr. McKinley.'

'Against me?' McKinley looked surprised. He eyed Waco, but appeared not to recognize him. 'And what might those charges be, sheriff?'

'Well, I . . . ' The big lawman shifted uncomfortably on his feet. 'Maybe we should discuss this somewhere a mite more private, sir. Inside, maybe?'

'Very well.' McKinley opened the door and stepped back so they could enter ahead of him. 'How about my study? No one will bother us there.'

Once in the large, comfortably-furnished study at the rear of the house, McKinley motioned for Waco and the sheriff to be seated and then indicated the bar facing one of the big windows overlooking the desert. 'What may I offer you to drink, gentlemen?'

'Nothing, thank you, sir,' Sheriff Forbes replied.

'Are you sure about that? I've just received several cases of very fine Scotch whiskey from my homeland. If I may be excused for bragging, it goes down like melted honey. Very well,' he continued when Waco and the sheriff shook their heads, 'a cigar then?'

Again, both men shook their heads.

'Well, I hope you won't mind if I indulge?' McKinley said with a touch of irritation. He took a cigar from a silver humidor and clipped off the tip. 'It's one of the few luxuries I allow myself in this godforsaken wilderness.' He fired a match with a flick of his thumbnail and then puffed away, taking his time lighting up. Finally satisfied, he exhaled a thin stream of smoke, sat in a large hide-covered armchair and beamed at them.

'Now, then, laddie,' he said to the sheriff, 'why don't you be so kind as to describe exactly what these imaginary charges are?'

Tired of McKinley's smooth talk, Waco said bluntly: 'They ain't imaginary, mister. They're as real as that cigar you're smoking.'

'Is that so?' McKinley lost his insipid smile and stared at Waco. 'Have we met before, Mr . . . uh, Waco, was it?'

'Damn right we have — at a lynching at Fuller's Oak, outside Mesilla.'

To McKinley's credit, his bland expression never changed. He blew smoke toward the beamed ceiling and then tapped the ash from his cigar into a tray beside his chair.

'Lynching? You must have me mistaken for someone else. I've never attended a lynching in my life.'

'You're a liar, McCutcheon!'

McKinley momentarily flinched then recovered. 'Who?'

'McCutcheon,' Waco repeated. 'Judd McCutcheon.'

McKinley calmly blew more cigar smoke at the ceiling and then shook his head. 'Sorry. You're definitely mistaken. I don't know who this McCutcheon is, but my name is and always has been Jory McKinley. Isn't that correct, sheriff?'

Sheriff Forbes hesitated and looked at Waco. 'Perhaps he's right,' he began.

Waco stopped him. 'He's *not* right! Goddammit, sheriff, can't you see he's lying?'

'Why would I lie about that?' McKinley asked. 'I'm no criminal or ex-con. And I haven't done anything illegal that would force me to change names.'

''Cept desert your son, wife and her daughter,' Waco said angrily.

'Now I *know* you're mistaking me for someone else,' McKinley said. 'I've never been married and I certainly don't have a son.' He turned to the sheriff. 'You've known me for quite a spell now, Lonnie. Have you ever heard anyone claim I was married? Or had children?'

The lawman grudgingly shook his head.

'Well, there you are then,' McKinley said. 'Now will you kindly tell this man to stop badgering me? I'm not who he thinks I am. What's more, I have no recollection of ever meeting him before, lynching or otherwise. Naturally, I've heard of Fuller's Oak. What person in New Mexico hasn't? But I assure you I've never had any reason to meet anyone at the so-called Hangman's Tree . . . '

'Well,' the sheriff said, 'I got no reason to doubt your word, Mr. McKinley, but — '

'I have!' Waco exclaimed. Ripping open his shirt, he showed McKinley the rope-burns around his neck. 'How about this for a goddamn reason?' Then as McKinley recoiled: 'Does this help 'jog' your memory, you lying sonofabitch?'

McKinley lost it. He angrily pushed Waco aside and rising, glared at the sheriff.

'Damn you, Forbes, I expected better from you than this kind of crass insinuating!'

'I ain't 'insinuating,'' Waco raged, 'I'm accusing you, you murdering bastard!'

The sheriff quickly pulled Waco away from McKinley and forced him to sit on the cowhide sofa. He then turned to McKinley, saying: 'I'd appreciate it if you'd sit too, sir.'

Once McKinley was seated, the sheriff faced both men.

'That's better,' he said, with more authority than Waco had expected. 'Now, I want both of you to listen carefully to what I got to say.' He waited until he was sure he had their undivided attention before continuing. 'As you can see, Mr. McKinley, there

176

ain't no doubting this fella's been hanged. That's undeniable. But who hanged him and when and where, well, that's when it gets a bit foggy.'

'Well, it sure as hell wasn't me,' McKinley snapped.

'Liar,' Waco said.

McKinley ignored him and continued talking to the lawman. 'If I'd stretched his neck, Lonnie, you can be damned sure that he wouldn't have lived to talk about it.'

'Like my brother, huh?' Waco threw in.

'Your brother?' McKinley frowned at him. 'Are you suggesting that I not only hung you, but your younger brother as well?'

Waco pounced. 'Who said it was my younger brother?'

'You just did.'

'Uh-uh. I just said brother. Ain't that so, sheriff?'

The big lawman thought a moment then nodded and looked suspiciously at McKinley. 'He's right, sir. He never mentioned if his brother was younger or older.'

'Which proves you're lying,' Waco told McKinley. ''Cause only someone who was there, at the lynching, would know Chris was younger than me.'

'That's ridiculous,' McKinley said. 'Even if I did mistakenly say he was younger, it was nothing more than a slip of the tongue. I could just as easily have said older brother. Neither mistake proves a blasted thing. And if you think it does,' he added to the sheriff, 'I suggest you arrest me and make a laughing stock of yourself in court!'

Sheriff Forbes chewed his lip uneasily.

'Dammit,' Waco erupted, 'don't turn weak-kneed on me now!'

The lawman reddened. 'Watch your mouth, son,' he warned. 'I got more than one empty cell waiting for a customer.'

'All right,' Waco said, calming, 'maybe you're right. Maybe we should play this cautiously.' Turning to McKinley, he added: 'Forget the lynching for a moment. How do you explain that both you and my brother were involved in rustling?'

'Rustling?' McKinley almost laughed. 'Don't be absurd. Why the devil would I steal cattle when I've a got a large herd of my own?'

''Cause half of your beef belongs to Mr. Stadtlander, that's why.'

'If you're talking about the hundred or so cows that wander onto my range every year, then I should remind you that an equal number of my cattle wander onto his range. It's all part of owning adjoining ranches . . . of trusting one another enough not to keep our herds from mingling by fencing our boundaries with Devil's Rope.'

'That's another lie,' said Waco. 'Reason you don't string barbed wire is 'cause it would hamper your rustling activities. And before you deny being a rustler again, McKinley or McCutcheon or whoever you are, what would you say if said I had definite proof I was right?'

'I'd say you were either a liar or delusional,' replied McKinley. Then to the sheriff: 'Lonnie, do we really have to continue this farce? I have no idea why this man is trying to invent trouble for me, but it's obvious he is or else he would show us this 'proof' that he claims to have and end this argument once and for all. But, of course, he can't do that because his so-called proof doesn't exist.'

'Sheriff,' Waco said quickly, 'don't let this murderer out of your sight.'

'Why? Where you going?'

'To get the proof that Mr. McKinley claims doesn't exist.'

''Mean that running iron you told me about?'

'Damn right,' Waco said. 'I'm betting it's right here on his property.' As he spoke he watched McKinley. The rancher did as Waco hoped and glanced uneasily at the barn. 'Be right back, sheriff.'

20

Confident that he was right, Waco entered the barn and looked about him, trying to decide where McKinley might have hidden the running iron. Grabbing a pitchfork, he tossed the hay aside in each of the three empty stalls, but came up empty. A chestnut mare was tied up in a fourth stall. Waco slapped it on the rump, forcing it to press against the wall. He then tossed aside the hay that covered the floor. Same result. Nothing!

Frustrated, Waco looked up at the pile of hay and sacks of grain that filled the loft. Going to the ladder, he climbed up to the loft and began searching amongst the straw. Again, he came up empty. He sighed, worried now that he might not be able to make good on his promise. He glanced about him. His gaze settled on a pile of grain sacks stacked in one corner. Wondering if the running iron was hidden behind them, Waco moved closer. It was then he noticed some of the sacks were stained. He felt one of the stains and realized the sacking was damp. Puzzled, he wondered why these particular sacks were damp when the others were not. Then it hit him. They'd been moved!

Quickly, he pulled the stained sacks aside. All of them were damp only on the sides where they had pressed against other sacks. Moving the last damp sack, he saw a glint of metal. He bent closer and realized it was the running iron.

Excited, he grabbed it and examined the brand. Even in the dimness of the loft, he saw that originally the brand had been Stadtlander's Double S. Someone had brazed a small iron loop to each tip of the S, turning it into the Lazy B. Feeling vindicated, Waco quickly descended the ladder and hurried out of the barn.

The sheriff and McKinley were still in the study — only now both were enjoying a drink poured from a bottle of Glengoyne single malt Scotch whiskey that according to the label had been established in 1833. Behind McKinley, a Sharps rifle hung on buck antlers above the stone fireplace.

Both men looked up as Waco entered, holding the running iron.

'Here you go, sheriff,' he said, setting the iron on the table between the two men. 'Maybe now you'll arrest this lying, murdering bastard!'

McKinley, who'd furtively slipped his hand inside his jacket when Waco entered, now pulled it out to reveal he was holding a Smith & Wesson single action .22 Short spur trigger pocket revolver.

'Somehow,' he said smugly, 'I don't think that's going to happen.'

'Go ahead and shoot,' Waco told him. 'You can't get off two shots before one of us kills you.'

'Granted,' McKinley agreed. 'But, small as this gun is, the one I do shoot is going to be very dead. So now all you have to decide is which one of you is willing to die for the other.' When neither man moved, McKinley rose, saying: 'What? No takers?' He laughed scornfully. 'So much for the myth idealizing the great American frontiersman! By God, when it boils down to dying, you're no more heroic than the rest of us.'

Waco didn't answer. He just stood there waiting his chance to strike.

'Now if you please,' McKinley continued, 'put your guns on the table and then step back where I can see you. Do it!' he snapped when they didn't move. 'Otherwise, I shall have to make the choice myself. And that would have to be — you,' he said, aiming his little revolver at the lawman. 'I've always disliked your ugly guts.'

Sheriff Forbes bottled his rage, drew his six-gun and set it on the table.

'Now you, Waco,' McKinley said. 'Your iron, as you call it, please.'

Waco slowly drew his Colt and started to set it on the table.

But at the last instant he brought his knee up under the table, sending it crashing into McKinley. The startled rancher staggered back, accidentally discharging the revolver.

Waco was on him immediately. His first punch sent McKinley sprawling. Dazed, he dropped his gun and offered no resistance as Waco dragged him up then knocked him flying again with a second punch.

'Wait,' Sheriff Forbes said as Waco went to haul McKinley up again, 'don't hog all the fun. The bastard was going to shoot me first, remember?' Jerking McKinley to his feet, the lawman knocked him to the floor. It was a devastating punch and the rancher landed in a crumpled heap and remained still.

'Now that,' the sheriff grinned, 'was a true pleasure.'

Waco went to the window and looked out. The hands were gathering outside, curious to know what was going on. Waco turned to the sheriff, saying:

'Reckon we'd better get this skunk away from here fast, 'fore his men decide to stomp us.'

The lawman nodded. Picking up the half-empty whiskey bottle, he forced open McKinley's mouth and poured the liquor into him. 'Foreigners,' he said, winking at Waco. 'Everyone knows they can't hold their whiskey.' Hoisting McKinley up, the sheriff threw him over his shoulder like a sack of wheat. 'Once we get outside,' he told Waco, 'if anybody asks us where we're going with their boss, tell 'em into town.'

Outside, the hands gathered around as they saw their boss with his arms draped about Waco and the sheriff's shoulders, all three men appearing to be pretty liquored up.

Waco yelled at one of the hands. 'Hey, you! Bring over that wagon.'

'Where you going with it?' the hand demanded.

'Santa Rosa.'

'It's my 50th birthday,' the sheriff

said. 'Your boss insists on celebrating with us.'

'Mr. McKinley,' the hand said, 'looks like he's already celebrated enough.'

The sheriff peered at McKinley, who was starting to come around. With his free hand the lawman lifted up the rancher's head. McKinley stared out at his men with a befuddled look on his bearded face.

'Maybe you should tell him that,' the sheriff said to the hand. 'Reckon he'd take right kindly to you telling him what he can and can't do.'

'Not me,' the hand said, backing away. 'I draw wages to punch cattle not give my boss orders.'

'How 'bout the rest of you?' the sheriff asked the other men.

None of them said anything.

By now the man Waco had spoken to had brought up the wagon. The sheriff picked McKinley up and sat him on the seat, then climbed up beside him and grabbed the reins.

Waco, meanwhile, tied the lawman's

horse to the rear of the wagon and mounted up.

'Oh, I almost forgot,' Sheriff Forbes told the hands. 'There's a case of mighty good Scotch whiskey in the study. Your boss said while he's in town, he wants you men to do a little celebrating of your own. Sort of a bonus for how hard you been working.'

For a moment the men couldn't believe their luck. Then, with whoops of joy, they crowded into the house.

The sheriff snapped the reins and the team pulled the wagon away, Waco riding alongside it.

'Know what?' he said as they reached the gate. 'I underestimated you, Lonnie.'

Sheriff Forbes chuckled. 'Don't sweat it, son. You ain't the first and you sure as hell won't be the last.'

21

The jolting ride in the wagon sobered McKinley enough for him to open his eyes and in a slurred voice ask where they were going. The sheriff drew his six-gun and slammed it against the rancher's head. McKinley slumped over his knees and would have fallen off the seat if Waco hadn't ridden close and pushed the unconscious Scotsman into the back of the moving wagon. He remained there, unconscious, until they reached Santa Rosa.

'You know what's going to happen when their boss doesn't come back to the ranch?' Waco said as he helped the lawman drag the semi-conscious McKinley out of the wagon and into the sheriff's office.

'Sure. They'll be riding in to find out what's happened to him.'

'Armed to the teeth,' added Waco.

'Don't forget that little detail.'

'I ain't forgetting nothing, Ace. But by then, McKinley will be locked in a cell and my deputies will have orders to shoot anyone who tries to break him out.'

'Deputy, don't you mean? A man who's a half-assed spittoon cleaner at best.'

'Wrong,' the sheriff corrected. 'I'm not counting on Farley. He's a worthless sack of pus like you said. But as soon as McKinley's behind bars, I'm swearing in as many volunteers as I can find, and then come daylight I'll be taking McKinley to Deming on the early train. There, I'll hand him over to the Federal Marshal, who'll keep him jailed till he's indicted and a trial date is set.'

Waco shook his head. 'That might work in one of Ned Buntline's dime novels, sheriff, but this is reality.'

'Meaning?'

'McKinley — or McCutcheon — is a snake who surrounds himself with other

190

snakes, namely professional gunmen from hellholes on both sides of the border. Most of them are scum who enjoy killing and burning and dynamiting to get whatever it is they want, which in this instance is their boss. And hiring a bunch of well-meaning citizens, who've probably never even drawn a gun in anger, let alone been in a gunfight, and asking them to go up against a bunch of cold-blooded shootists is — well, like asking a young'un to fight a grizzly.'

'I think you're misjudging folks around here,' the sheriff said. 'Sure, they're bankers and storekeepers now, but back in the day, most of them fought against Indians, outlaws and Comancheros — even Union troops — and still came out victorious.'

'You're talking about the older folks,' Waco argued, ' — settlers, who came out here in the '60s and early '70s. That's almost 30 years ago. They're now in their fifties or sixties.'

'I'm fifty,' Sheriff Forbes said, 'and I

can still handle a gun with the best of 'em.'

'You're a lawman, so that makes you an exception. I'm talking about townspeople — shopkeepers and barbers and the like. Are you willing to risk your life on their gunplay?'

The big lawman shrugged. 'Okay,' he said. 'If you got a better plan, let's hear it.'

'It ain't a plan so much as simple deception.'

'Keep talking.'

'Only way to keep McCutcheon in custody is to outsmart his men. Make them think you got their boss locked up in jail, when actually you're taking him to Deming tonight.'

'There ain't no train to Deming tonight.'

'I know that,' Waco said. 'But a train ain't the only way to get to Deming.'

'Maybe not. But if I take him there on horseback or in a wagon, everyone in town will see us, including folks who count McKinley as their friend. One of 'em's bound to let his men know right away and — '

Waco stopped him. 'Who said anything about horseback or wagon?'

'Well, what other way is there?' the sheriff demanded.

Waco grinned. 'Follow me,' he said. 'I'll explain along the way.'

22

By the light of a coal-oil lamp Carson Wood finished planing the edges of the coffin he was building and began sandpapering the roughened wood until every splinter was gone. Just to be sure, he ran his palm over the edges. Then, satisfied it was perfectly smooth, he wiped the sweat from his brow and picked up the lid. Placing it on the empty coffin, he checked the fit. Most morticians would have been delighted by how well it fit, but Carson was not like most morticians. A master carpenter by trade, he'd only become an undertaker because the prior mortician had suddenly died of blackwater fever and the town fathers, terrified that the disease might spread, had quickly burned his corpse and clothing and buried him outside the cemetery. They then advertised for another mortician in the local and neighboring towns' newspapers. A month passed and no one answered. Desperate, and with two more corpses on ice, the mayor approached Carson. He agreed to help out, but only on a temporary basis — until a trained mortician could be found.

But then an odd thing happened: in the weeks that followed Carson discovered that he enjoyed his new line of work better than carpentry, and after learning the ropes from an elderly, retired undertaker in Deming, he'd returned to Santa Rosa and taken over the dead mortician's business. A big-chested, strong man with thinning blond hair, merry blue eyes and a booming laugh, he looked more like a blacksmith than an undertaker. But the townspeople liked him and Carson attacked his new job with his usual enthusiasm.

Now, as he sanded the last bit of roughness from the edges of the coffin lid he heard someone enter his store and went inside to greet them. Surprised to see his 'customers' were Sheriff Forbes and a tall lean cowboy he'd never met, he asked what they wanted.

'Before I answer that,' the sheriff replied, 'I first want your word that what I'm about to say is in the strictest confidence.'

''Mean you want to keep this funeral a secret?'

'You could put it that way,' the sheriff said wryly. 'Now do I got your word?'

'Absolutely,' Carson said. 'Whatever you say will go to my grave with me.'

'Good. Then here's what I need. I want to rent your hearse for two — no, make that three days, and one of your coffins.'

'Rent?' Carson frowned, confused. 'You can't rent a coffin, Lonnie. Once it's buried in the ground, it can't be dug up and used again. By then it's rotted and full of worms — '

'We're not burying it and the fella who's in it will be alive.'

Carson looked even more confused. 'Let me get this straight. Are you saying the deceased — I mean the person you want buried isn't dead yet?'

'That's exactly what I'm saying. Now, is your hearse available and do you have a coffin ready to go?'

'Sure. I fed the team this morning and I got several coffins already built. You just got to choose the one best suited for your needs.'

'It has to be big enough for someone roughly my size to fit in it,' Waco said, adding: 'Oh yeah, and we need you to drill several holes in the lid.'

'H-Holes?'

'Uh-huh.'

'How big do you want them — the holes, I mean?'

'Big enough so the person inside can breathe through them,' the sheriff said.

Still confused, Carson decided not to argue with the law. Instead, he said: 'I'll have to charge you extra for the holes, sheriff.'

'Why's that?'

''Cause when you bring the coffin back, I got to make a new lid.'

'Fair enough,' the sheriff agreed. 'Just mark it down on the bill, so I got something to show the town fathers.'

'Will do,' Carson promised. Then: 'One last thing. When do you need my hearse?'

'Yesterday,' Sheriff Forbes said wryly. 'But I'll settle for thirty minutes.'

'I better get started drilling them holes then,' Carson said.

'Oh, and when you're done,' Waco said, 'put the coffin in the hearse, then bring the hearse around to the rear of the jail and leave it there.'

'Then go back to your store and act like nothing unusual has happened. Okay?' the sheriff said.

Carson nodded.

'And not a word to anybody. Got it?'

'Not a living soul. I swear.'

'Good man.'

23

Thirty minutes later Waco looked out the back door of the jail and saw a black, glass-sided hearse tied to a tree. It was harnessed to two mules with red plumes atop their heads and the inner curtains were drawn, preventing anyone from seeing inside.

'All clear,' Waco told the sheriff. 'Bring the sonofabitch out.'

Moments later Sheriff Forbes emerged with a bound and gagged McKinley over his shoulder. By then Waco already had the back of the hearse open, revealing an empty coffin with the lid off. The two of them quickly put McKinley into the coffin and closed the lid. Waco peered through one of the three holes drilled in the lid. McKinley's eyes glared back at him. Seeing Waco further infuriated the rancher. He fought desperately to get free, his cursing muffled by the gag.

'Go ahead,' Waco told him. 'Struggle all you want, you bastard. I tied them knots myself. You ain't got a hope in hell of getting loose.' Jumping off the hearse, he closed the door and turned to the sheriff. 'Better get going 'fore McCutcheon's men show up.'

The lawman nodded. 'Now remember what I told you. When they get here, threaten to arrest them if they don't leave peacefully . . . but try not to shoot any of them.'

'Thought that's why you deputized me?'

'I deputized you so you had a legal right to represent me and defend yourself. Not so you could use folks for target practice.'

'This filth ain't 'folks',' Waco said. 'Like I told you, they're nothing but hired gunmen! The dregs of the dregs — ' He broke off as the church bell started ringing, then added: 'That's Farley. Get moving!'

The sheriff quickly jumped up on the seat and cracked his whip. The mules lunged ahead, pulling the fancy-looking hearse along the dark alley running behind the buildings.

Waco ducked back inside the jail and locked the heavy door behind him. Entering the office, he grabbed a shotgun and a Winchester from the gun rack and made sure they were loaded. He then carried them outside and looked up and down Main Street. It was almost dark now and lights showed in all the cantinas and the stores that were still open.

Waco leaned the guns against the wall and told all the passersby to get off the street and go home. He offered no explanation but his grim expression was enough for the people not to question his orders, and they hurried off.

Waco sighed, angry with himself for getting involved in a potential gunfight that he could have avoided merely by riding straight to McKinley's — or McCutcheon's — ranch and shooting him on the spot. Yeah, he reminded himself. But then he wouldn't have found out that his brother was indeed rustling cattle and deserved to be imprisoned or even hung for his crime. On the other hand, he argued, Chris wouldn't have been lynched by a mob out for blood, and he, Waco, wouldn't have been permanently scarred with rope burns!

But there was a good side to it too: if he hadn't come to Santa Rosa he wouldn't have met Georgina Lockhart! Oh, sure, it was foolish to think about her or his future with her in the position that he was in right now. But he couldn't help it. She'd made a huge impression on him, and he promised himself that if he was still alive after dealing with McCutcheon's gunfighters, he would not ride off without seeing if she was as interested in him as much as he was interested in —

His thoughts were interrupted by a tall, thin man who rushed up to him, gasping for air, blurting: 'Th-they're a-coming, sheriff! Yes they are, indeed they are, I saw 'em myself, yes I did.'

'I reckoned they were,' Waco replied, 'when I heard you ringing the bell.'

'M-Must be twenty or thirty of 'em, yes there are!'

'How far away?'

''Bout a mile, yes, sir, a mile or maybe less, sheriff.'

'You don't have to call me sheriff, Farley,' Waco said. 'I'm just a deputy like you.'

'Maybe so, but Sheriff Forbes, he told me I was to obey everything you said, yes he did, so you just tell me what you want me to do and I'll jump right on it and — '

'Whoa, take a breath, okay? Calm down or you won't be no use to me at all.'

'Yes, sir, I'll do just that, yes I will, I'll take a breath.' Farley Rosebush collapsed on the hard-backed chair that always sat outside the sheriff's office and tried to regain his wind. Though he was now thirty-one, he wasn't intelligent enough to hold down steady work, unless it was very menial, and would never have been made a deputy if his aunt wasn't Sheriff Forbes' first cousin and — more importantly — the mayor's wife. But if nothing else he was eager and willing and obedient, and capable of making coffee and sweeping out the sheriff's office; and other than when the local children were taunting him, he always managed to be happy.

Looking at him now, Waco realized the kindest way to describe this simpleton was to say he was a child in a man's body and let it go at that. But there was one thing Waco had to know — and he had to know it now. 'Farley,' he said patiently, 'I'm going to ask you a question and I want you to answer it truthfully. Reckon you can do that?'

'Yes, sir, oh yes, I can do that easy. What's the question, sheriff?'

'Can you shoot?'

'Yes, sir. I can indeed shoot, yes I can. 'Course, I ain't allowed to carry a gun, but — '

'What if I gave you a gun — a rifle

— could you shoot it?'

'Yes, sir, I could, indeed I could. I could hit — '

'No, no, you don't need to *hit* anything, Farley.'

'I don't?'

'Uh-uh. All you got to do — and only if I ask you to — is shoot up in the air . . . above folks' heads.'

'I can do that, sheriff, yes I can. I can do that easy.' Farley paused, frowning as if puzzled, then like a kid unable to believe he was getting a Christmas present, said: 'You'd really give me a rifle, sheriff, would you?'

'Maybe,' Waco said. 'Depends on what McCutcheon's men do once they hit town.'

'McCutcheon?'

'I mean McKinley,' corrected Waco. Deciding not to further confuse Farley by explaining that McKinley and McCutcheon were one and the same, he added: 'One other thing. And this is important, Farley, so try to remember it, okay?'

'Yes, sir, sheriff, I will. Yes, indeed I will. What is it, sir?'

'I want McKinley's men to think that their boss is locked up in one of the cells.'

'But he ain't, sheriff, he's — '

'Never mind if he is or isn't,' Waco snapped. 'Just do as I tell you. And I'm *telling* you that I want McKinley's men to think their boss is locked in our jail. Got that?'

'In our jail, yes, sir, I got that, yes I have.'

'And when they demand that we let him go,' Waco continued, 'and I refuse, they're going to get angry and threaten to break him out. Do you understand that, Farley?'

'Yes, sir, yes I do. Indeed I do.'

'Good. Then understand this too. The longer we can hold them off the better.'

'Hold them off, sheriff?'

'Stop them from breaking in here and seeing that we don't have McKinley in jail. The longer we can do that, the safer it will be for Sheriff Forbes.'

''Mean he'll be in jail too?'

Waco almost lost it. But forcing himself to remain calm, he said patiently: 'No, Farley. The sheriff is on his way to Deming, remember? In that hearse we rented from Carson Whitfield, the undertaker.'

'Oh yeah, yeah, hearse, I remember, yes I do, the one with the black curtains and the bright red feathers on the mules' heads?'

'That's the one. But that's our little secret. You're not to tell McKinley's men anything about the hearse. Understand?'

'Y-Yes, sir, I understand, I . . . no, not really.'

'It's simple, Farley. If McKinley's men find out their boss is in that hearse, they will ride after the sheriff and when they overtake him, they'll stop him from taking McKinley to Deming. Maybe even shoot him. And we don't want that, do we, Farley?'

Farley shook his head. 'No, sir, no,

we don't want that at all, we sure don't, oh no.'

Waco, worn out from explaining, looked up the street as he heard horses coming. He couldn't see the riders yet, since the street lights only lit up Main Street. But by the noise of their hooves he knew it would only be a matter of minutes before the horsemen came busting into town with only one thought in mind: to find their boss and take him back to his ranch.

And when that happened, Waco knew that no amount of explaining would stop them from tearing the sheriff's office apart . . . and possibly even Santa Rosa as well!

24

Waco made sure that all the citizens had obeyed his orders about getting off Main Street and then told Farley to go into the sheriff's office and stay there. 'Once you're inside,' he added, 'stand to one side of the window. Then, if you hear me tap on the glass, break the window and fire over the heads of McKinley's men. You understand me, Farley? Over their heads!'

'Yes, sir, oh yes, I understand, indeed I do.'

'Then repeat what I told you.'

Farley screwed up his face as he tried to remember.

'Best tell me again, sheriff, so's I remember exactly, yes sir.'

Waco patiently repeated the instructions.

Farley then repeated them, word for word, and when he was finished he beamed happily. 'Did I say 'em right, sheriff, did I, did I?'

'You sure did,' Waco said. 'Now, get inside and don't do anything until you hear me tap on the window.'

Waco waited until Farley was safely in the sheriff's office. Then he sat on the chair, shotgun across his lap, rifle within easy reach and waited.

It was full-on dark now, save for the lights, and the approaching riders had reached Main Street. Waco could hear them coming toward him from both ends of the street. He knew they were making sure that the sheriff couldn't escape with their boss. Though it had grown cold Waco felt his palms sweating. Telling himself to calm down and relax, he thumbed back both hammers on the double-barreled shotgun but still didn't lift it from his lap. He'd known many lawmen over the years, some famous, others unknown, and though each one handled danger differently, they all agreed on one thing: no matter how scared you were, never show fear.

The riders were close enough now for him to see their outlines in the darkness. Farley had been right: there was at least twenty men and every one of them a professional killer. What was even more unsettling: a lot of their victims had been lawmen!

Waco leisurely rolled a cigarette, lit it and inhaled a lungful of smoke. As he slowly exhaled, McKinley's men reined up in front of him. All heavily armed, they were led by Box Wilson, a sadistic illiterate gunman who had a reputation for raping the wives and daughters of men he gunned down and then torching their homes.

Box grinned as he saw Waco seated in front of him. 'Well, now,' he rasped. 'Reckon my ol' man was right after all. Everything does come to him who waits.'

Waco calmly sucked in another satisfying lungful of smoke and flipped his cigarette away. He then lifted up the shotgun and pointed both barrels at the leering gunman.

'Box, unless you want to end up like your brother did in Laredo turn your men around and get the hell out of town.'

'Not till the goddamn sheriff hands over our boss.'

'That ain't going to happen, Box, and you know it.'

'I want to hear Sheriff Forbes say that. Where is he?'

'Inside with the prisoner.'

'Then tell him this: If he don't release Mr. McKinley right now, we'll bust in and take him by force . . . and gun down you and the sheriff while we're at it.'

'You'll try, you mean.'

Box laughed. 'Hell, Waco, you plan on stopping us all by your lonesome?'

'Maybe not all of you,' Waco said, keeping the shotgun trained on Box. 'But I'll sure as hell stop you — and anyone close to you.'

The gunmen on either side of Box immediately nudged their horses away.

'Go ahead, *hombre*. But remember this: while you're blasting me, my boys will be slinging lead your way.'

'And the sheriff's deputies will be returning the favor.'

'Deputies?' Box chuckled contemptuously. 'What deputies?'

Instead of answering Waco tapped on the window beside him. Nothing happened. Waco tapped again, harder.

This time the window suddenly shattered and a rifle poked out. Broken glass rained down on the boardwalk, startling the gunmen's horses.

'Satisfied?' Waco asked Box.

Box started to reply — but his words were lost as Farley started firing shots over the heads of McKinley's men. His aim was shaky and the bullets came uncomfortably close to the gunmen, forcing them to wheel their horses around and scatter.

Waco saw Box reaching for his Colt and fired at him. But by then Box was already a moving target and the buckshot missed him and killed the gunman next to him. Man and horse crashed to the ground, adding to the chaos . . .

Waco ducked into the sheriff's office and kicked the door shut.

Farley grinned at him from beside the broken window. 'I done what you asked me, sheriff, yes sir, I broke the glass and fired over them fellas' heads, yes, sir, I sure did.'

Waco started to reply but instead had to hit the floor as Box and his men opened fire. A storm of bullets poured in through the window, shattering the remaining glass.

'Should I keep firing?' Farley shouted. 'Should I, sheriff, should I?'

'Yeah,' Waco replied, scrambling to the opposite side of the window. 'But now start shooting *at* those bastards, not over their heads!'

'Oh, boy,' Farley said, beaming. 'This'll be fun, yes sir, it sure will be, lots of fun, won't it be fun, sheriff?'

Waco didn't bother to reply. Crawling to the gun rack, he opened the top drawer and grabbed several boxes of cartridges.

'Here,' he said, throwing two boxes to Farley. 'Try to make every shot count.'

'I'll try, yes I will,' Farley said. Then as it hit him: 'B-But I can't count, sheriff.'

Waco rolled his eyes. 'That's okay,' he said. 'Just keep shooting and trying to hit someone.' He ducked as more bullets zipped past his head. They ricocheted around the office, leaving silvery streaks wherever they touched and ended up punching holes in the rear wall. Waco poked his gun out the side of the window, took quick aim at a gunman crouched behind a post on the opposite boardwalk and fired. The man pitched onto his face and for a few moments lay twitching in the street, his blood staining the dirt.

Waco picked off another gunman the same way and then had to pull back and flatten himself against the wall as the infuriated gunmen returned fire. Their bullets chewed at the framework around the window until gradually the window sill was destroyed and the last pieces of glass fell out and shattered on the boardwalk.

There was a sudden lull in the shooting.

Waco peered around the damaged woodwork and saw several gunmen were now pushing an empty freight wagon toward the sheriff's office. They kept the wagon between them and Waco, using it as cover so that neither he nor Farley could shoot them.

'Farley!' he yelled at the deputy. 'Follow me!' Ducked low, he ran to the desk and with Farley's help dragged it to the door leading back to the cell area. Together they turned the desk on its side and ducked behind it.

Farley beamed, childlike, at him. 'I sure wish you was sheriff, yes I do, I surely do, 'cause Sheriff Forbes, he treats me like he wishes I wasn't here, yes, sir, he does indeed.'

'That's 'cause he's got a lot more responsibility than me,' was all Waco could think to say. 'But he thinks you're a good deputy.'

'He does?' Farley frowned, surprised.

'You bet. Told me so lots of — ' Waco broke off as the wagon tongue suddenly smashed through the front door, breaking the lock and the hinges so that the skewered door collapsed inward.

Waco immediately opened fire at the gunmen who came pouring in. His bullets cut down the first few men, the others behind them stumbling over their dead bodies.

Farley squealed with delight and pumped round after round into the onrushing gunmen. His bullets killed or wounded several of them but still they kept busting in, firing as they came, their bullets splintering the desk shielding Waco and Farley.

Simultaneously there was an explosion at the rear of the building. Waco whirled around in time to see the rest of the gunmen entering through the demolished back door.

'Throw down your gun,' Waco told

Farley. 'You hear me?' he added when the deputy didn't obey. 'Drop your rifle 'fore they kill you.'

Grudgingly, Farley obeyed.

'Now stand up and raise your hands like this,' Waco said, holding up his hands. 'And whatever they tell you to do, do it. Understand?'

Farley nodded, and like a scolded child held up both hands.

25

Box elbowed his way through the men and angrily confronted Waco. 'Give me the keys to the cells,' he demanded.

'I don't have them,' Waco said. 'The sheriff keeps them on his belt at all times.'

Box eyed the locked door blocking his way to the cells then glared at Waco. 'Tell him to open the door.'

'You tell him. He might listen to you.'

Box drew his six-gun and pounded on the door with the butt. 'Sheriff? Sheriff Forbes, can you hear me?'

No answer.

'You got ten seconds to open that goddamn door or I'll blast it open!'

No answer.

Box turned to one of his men and stuck out his hand. The man pulled a stick of dynamite from the sack he was carrying and gave it to Box. The gunman scratched a match on his belt buckle and lit the fuse. He then placed the burning stick on the floor next to the door and waved everyone back. As one, the gunmen scrambled out the rear door. Waco started after them and then stopped as he saw that Farley hadn't moved.

'C'mon!' Waco hissed at him. 'Hurry, goddammit!'

If Farley heard Waco, he didn't show it. He just stood there, fascinated, happily watching the fuse burn, a look of pure joy on his childlike face.

Cursing, Waco grabbed Farley's arm, saying 'C'mon, damn you!' and dragged the simple-minded deputy out into the alley. There, they ducked behind the wall facing the sheriff's office, joining Box and the other gunmen huddled there.

Moments later the dynamite exploded with a deafening roar. The explosion blew a giant hole in the rear of the jail, debris flying everywhere. Before even the dust settled, Box and his men, guns in hand, herded Waco and Farley to the gaping hole.

'Keep 'em covered,' Box told one gunman. 'If they try to make a break for it, shoot 'em.'

He then led the rest of the men in through the hole.

Waco took a deep breath, knowing what was going to happen next. He looked at Farley and winked. The deputy beamed as if he'd just been let in on a secret.

Moments later Box angrily reappeared and stormed up to Waco. 'I ought to gun you down right here and now,' he snarled.

'Listen,' Waco said, 'if you killed your own boss, don't blame me. You're the damn fool who used dyna — '

Box angrily clubbed him with his Colt, dropping Waco where he stood. 'Pick him up,' Box barked at his men. Two of them obeyed and held the still-dazed Waco between them. Box grabbed his shirt and pulled him close. 'Where the hell is he?' he demanded.

'You better start talking,' he warned when Waco didn't answer, ''cause if you don't tell me where Mr. McKinley is in the next five seconds, I'm going to shoot this idiot you call a deputy!' He pressed his gun against Farley's temple. 'Five . . . four . . . three — '

'Sheriff Forbes got him,' Waco blurted.

'Got him where?'

'By now, I reckon they're halfway to Deming.'

Box backhanded him across the face. 'Lying sonofabitch,' he snarled. 'There's no train to Deming till morning.'

'They ain't taking the train,' Waco said, licking the blood from his lips. 'Sheriff's got your boss tied up in a hearse. They took off long before you hit town.'

Farley suddenly giggled. 'Ain't nothing you can do 'bout it neither, no sir, nothing at all, not one littlest thing.' He beamed, pleased with himself. 'Sheriff outfoxed you, that's what he done all right, yes, sir, he outfox — '

Enraged, Box shot him.

For an instant Farley stood there, a bewildered expression on his gaunt, wide-eyed face, blood staining his shirt above his heart. Then he crumpled and lay in a lifeless heap.

Waco erupted. 'You no-good, cowardly, murdering sonofabitch!' he raged at Box. 'If it's the last goddamn thing I do, I'll see you hang for this!'

'You won't live that long,' Box growled. He went to shoot Waco — when a shot rang out behind him. He stumbled forward, looking as stunned and bewildered as Farley had moments earlier, and then collapsed on his face. Dead.

Waco and the gunmen whirled around and saw Georgie and her son Mason, who was carrying a Winchester single shot rifle, advancing along the dark alley. Directly behind them, also armed, followed an angry crowd of townspeople.

'Looks like you scum have outstayed

your welcome,' Waco told the gunmen. 'If I were you, I'd high-tail it back across the border where you belong. You got no dog in this fight anymore.'

'He's right,' agreed one of the gunmen. 'Let's ride.' The others needed no urging. Holstering their guns, they hurried into the sheriff's office and on out to Main Street, where they quickly mounted and rode off.

By now Georgie, Mason and the townspeople had crowded around Waco, eager to thank him. He quickly silenced them and pointed at Farley's corpse. 'He's the one you should be thanking, folks.'

The townspeople exchanged puzzled looks.

'Farley Rosebush?' the mayor said incredulously.

'That's right,' Waco said. 'No matter what you thought of him, he came through when he was needed. Always remember that. Always remember too that without Farley, I couldn't have held off those gunmen. They would've

found out right away that Sheriff
Forbes was taking McKinley to Deming
and hunted them down. What's more,
after they'd forced the sheriff to turn
over his prisoner, I reckon they
would've killed him. Farley's the reason
that didn't happen and it cost him his
life. His life, folks. So make sure he gets
the kind of funeral he deserves, 'long
with a headstone befitting a hero.'

Without waiting for the crowd to
respond, Waco pulled Georgie and
Mason aside and thanked the boy for
saving his life. Mason didn't answer and
wouldn't look at Waco.

'He's got something to tell you,'
Georgie said. Then to Mason: 'Go
ahead, Mace.'

Still refusing to look at Waco, Mason
shifted uncomfortably on his feet for a
few moments before finally muttering:
'Sorry I was rude to you, mister.'

Waco grinned. 'Reckon you've more
than made up for that, son.'

'There,' Georgie told Mason. 'That
wasn't so hard now, was it?'

Mason ignored her and continued looking at his feet.

'That's a mighty handsome rifle you got there,' Waco said when Mason didn't respond. 'Model '85 isn't it?'

Mason nodded and for the first time looked at Waco. 'Belonged to my pa. He give it to me for my birthday, 'bout a month 'fore he . . . he . . . ' He paused, unable to admit that his father had deserted him, then said: 'He taught me how to shoot it, too.'

'I'm glad he did,' Waco said. 'Else we wouldn't be having this little conversation.'

To Georgie he added: 'I been thinking. I know we ain't known each other too long. But I got some savings in a bank in Laredo. If you'd be willing, ma'am — '

'Georgie — '

' — Georgie, I'd like to invest it in your rooming house.'

'Invest it?' she said, surprised. 'How?'

'Seems to me you once said you still owed the bank money on it.'

226

'My mortgage, you mean?'

Waco nodded and, like Mason earlier, uncomfortably scuffed the dirt with his foot.

'And you want to pay that off?' Georgie said. 'Is that what you're saying?'

'Yeah. And if there's any money left over, maybe paint the place, spruce it up some . . . repair anything that needs fixing. That's if you'd be agreeable, of course.'

Georgie hesitated, mind churning, and then said: 'Well, I . . . might be.'

'Would you 'least give it some thought?' Waco said. 'I ain't pressing for an answer right away. But this town is growing mighty fast and a boarding house like yours, once it's all fixed up, well, I reckon it could be a regular gold mine for you — '

'For us,' she corrected. 'You and me.'

'Oh, no, ma'am, I didn't mean for it to sound like — '

'I'd never agree to it any other way,' Georgie said firmly.

'Y-You wouldn't?'

'Not for a second.'

Waco couldn't believe his ears. Or his luck.

'Okay,' he said, trying not to sound too eager. 'Reckon it's all settled then.' He extended his hand. Georgie started to shake it and then hesitated.

'Before I agree, Waco, there's something else you should know first.'

'What's that?' he asked uneasily.

'Last night, my daughter and I had a long much-needed talk.'

'Ma,' Mason tugged on her sleeve, 'Danny said not to tell nobody.'

'I know,' Georgie said. 'But circumstances change and I believe Mr. McAllum has a right to hear this.' Turning back to Waco, she added: 'Daniella made it very clear that she wants me to get married as soon as possible.'

'She didn't say as soon as possible, ma,' Mason corrected, 'she said 'right away'.'

Georgie ignored him and went on

talking to Waco. 'Of course, I tried to explain that it wasn't easy for a widow with children to find a man willing to shoulder that sort of responsibility, but, as usual, Daniella had her mind made up and wouldn't listen. She just kept on insisting that I wasn't trying hard enough.' Georgie paused and was silent so long that finally Mason tugged on her sleeve again and said: 'Ma, tell him the rest.'

Georgie hesitated and then saw enough interest in Waco's eyes to continue. 'Well, normally I wouldn't have let what she was saying bother me. Daniella can be an awful pest at times, but deep down she means well, and generally has my best interest at heart. So I usually just ignore her and go on about my business. But this time was . . . different.'

'Different?' Waco repeated. 'How?'

'I sensed that something was truly bothering her. Naturally, I asked her what it was. But she wouldn't tell me. I kept pressuring her, insisting that she tell me, and finally she admitted that once I was married she could go back to being a girl again.'

Waco frowned. 'I don't understand.'

'Neither did I. But Mason did.' Georgie turned to her stepson, saying: 'Tell him, Mace. Tell him what you told me.'

Mason gave a painful sigh, as if embarrassed by what he was going to say, and then said: 'It's all my pa's fault, Mr. McAllum. Right 'fore he run off and left us, he told Danny that she was the reason he got drunk all the time. 'Course, that got her all upset, and she begged him to explain why he blamed her. Pa said it was 'cause she was a girl. He then said that every father — hers included — dreamed of having sons, not daughters, 'cause daughters were nothing but a bunch of useless, whining, weepy girls.'

Waco, barely able to believe what he'd heard, didn't say anything.

'Unfortunately,' Georgie added, 'instead of ignoring what this dreadful